MY MIAMI 1992 JANUARY - NEW YEAR, NEW DRAMA

KRISTINA KASENGULU

MY MIAMI 1992 - JANUARY (NEW YEAR, NEW DRAMA)

Copyright © 2021 Kristina Kasengulu

All rights reserved. No part of this publication may be reproduced, stored in a retrieval system, or transmitted in any form or by any means, electronic, mechanical, photocopying, recording, or otherwise, without written permission of the author and publisher.

Published by Kristina Kasengulu, Edmonton, Canada

ISBN
Paperback 978-1-7776479-7-1
eBook 978-1-7776479-6-4

Digitally printed in Canada by
PAGEMASTER PUBLISHING
PageMasterPublishing.ca

MY MIAMI 1992 - JANUARY (NEW YEAR, NEW DRAMA)

DEDICATION

I dedicate this book to: My loving Mom, my hardworking Aunt Rose Joshua, my sweet brother Christophe, and my best friends Sara and Kaydence.

MY MIAMI 1992 - JANUARY (NEW YEAR, NEW DRAMA)

CONTENTS

Acknowledgments   5

Wednesday, January 1st, 1992   7
Thursday, January 2nd, 1992   18
Friday, January 3rd, 1992   21
Saturday, January 4th, 1992   28
Sunday, January 5th, 1992   31
Monday, January 6th, 1992   38
Tuesday, January 7th, 1992   46
Wednesday, January 8th, 1992   56
Thursday, January 9th, 1992   59
Friday, January 10th, 1992   64
Saturday, January 11th, 1992   68
Sunday, January 12th, 1992   70
Monday, January 13th, 1992   74
Tuesday, January 14th, 1992   81
Wednesday, January 15th, 1992   87
Thursday, January 16th, 1992   90
Friday, January 17th, 1992   95
Saturday, January 18th, 1992   98
Sunday, January 19th, 1992   100
Monday, January 20th, 1992   102
Tuesday, January 21st, 1992   107
Wednesday, January 22nd, 1992   109
Thursday, January 23rd, 1992   114
Friday, January 24th, 1992   117
Saturday, January 25th, 1992   123
Sunday, January 26th, 1992   137
Monday, January 27th, 1992   148
Tuesday, January 28th, 1992   151
Wednesday, January 29th, 1992   155
Thursday, January 30th, 1992   160
Friday, January 31st, 1992   162

MY MIAMI 1992 - JANUARY (NEW YEAR, NEW DRAMA)

ACKNOWLEDGEMENTS

None of this would be possible without the grace of God. Psalm 7:17 says "*I will give thanks to the Lord because of his righteousness; I will sing the praises of the name of the Lord Most High*." The Lord's faithfulness is the reason why I was able to create and publish this book. I am forever grateful, and His praises will forever stay in my mouth.

I'd like to express my gratitude to Dr. Rose Joshua (who I refer to as Aunty Rose). Words cannot express how grateful I am for all your efforts on this project, as well as your insightful ideas and faith in my visions. May God bless you and your family.

This project couldn't have been done without the love and support of my mom. Her wise counsel has been invaluable throughout this journey, and I have learned so much.

Finally, I'd like to thank Mr. Sieben, my fifth and sixth grade English teacher. He ignited a light in me and is the reason why I became interested in writing in the first place. Thank you for making me fall in love with literature!

MY MIAMI 1992 - JANUARY (NEW YEAR, NEW DRAMA)

MY MIAMI 1992 - JANUARY (NEW YEAR, NEW DRAMA)

Wednesday, January 1st, 1992

"3,2,1… Happy new year!" The whole room shouted. So much had transpired when the clock struck twelve midnight, I thought my head was going to explode! First, my dad popped open a large bottle of champagne; second, my 17-year-old brother Martin began to scream hysterically; third, my best friend, Meghan Benjaminson, squeezed me into a suffocating hug; fourth, fireworks blasted loudly outside; and finally, fifth, Mrs. Benjaminson (Meghan's mom) began to take 'millions' of images with her instant camera per second! Five things happening at the same time? This was crazy.

However, in a weird way it reminded me of the previous year, 1991, how so much had happened. Much that I was grateful for happened (like taking a super long road trip to Tampa, Florida) and some things that I wasn't so grateful for (like losing my grandfather to heart disease) happened as well, but it was now a new year. I had to remember the past, but also investigate the future – a new year, 1992.

"It's 1992! Jennifer! It's 1992!" Meghan squealed with delight. I too was quite thrilled that it was a new year, but I needed to catch a breath from Meghan's tight and uncomfortable hug.

"Meghan, if you don't let go of me now, I don't think I'll be able to see another minute of this year!" I managed to say loudly.

Meghan half smiled at me and let go.

MY MIAMI 1992 - JANUARY (NEW YEAR, NEW DRAMA)

"Happy new year, Jen," she said both happily and awkwardly at the same time.

"Same to you, Meg," I coughed, trying to catch back my breath.

I rubbed my arm. It was probably the most uncomfortable hug I had ever experienced in a while. A hug that was supposed to feel warm and lighthearted, but instead felt forced and a bit overbearing. Meghan had never hugged me like that before. Weird.

Suddenly, Martin interrupted my thoughts, walked over to me, and punched me in the arm playfully (although it did not feel very playful).

"Ow!" I screeched.

"Happy new year squirt," Martin teased.

"Your new year's resolution should be to stop calling me that," I shot back at him. I watched in annoyance as my rude and prideful brother simply chuckled to himself and walked away.

Meghan grabbed my arm (again with her unsettling grip) and led me to my family's living room window. We watched the fireworks in silence. It was beautiful.

Mrs. B came over from taking pictures of the parents to get a few pictures of the fireworks, then of Meghan and me together. We waited patiently for the pictures to be printed out of the instant camera slot (Mrs. B's camera was very old, so it often

MY MIAMI 1992 - JANUARY (NEW YEAR, NEW DRAMA)

took a while to print). Five images printed out, so we each got a picture of ourselves and the fireworks, and Mrs. B kept the fifth one for her own family pictures.

After family photographs and prayer over the new year, it was time for the parents to leave to go to our neighbor's house for more New Year festivities. Which meant Martin was going to be watching over us. Great.

By now you are probably wondering who I am, how old I am, where I'm from, and other things. Well, first off, my name is Jennifer, Jennifer Alexis Chevrolet (but my friends call me Jen). I'm a 5'3, twelve-year-old girl, in the seventh grade. I'm a natural brunette (my entire family is) and often get told I look older than I actually am. My mother always said that it was because I had a more mature looking face for my age.
I live in Coconut Grove, Miami, Florida. Don't get me wrong, I love Miami, I've lived in the Grove all my life, but the city is highly overrated. From how unreasonably expensive it is for my low-income family to the daily heatwaves and crazy traffic; I definitely did not believe it was the dream city everyone outside Miami portrayed it to be.

Besides all the expenses and everyday heatwaves my family and I experience in Miami, it wasn't so bad once you got used to it. I lived with my mom, dad, and older brother Martin. We live in a tiny condominium with three rooms, a singular bathroom, and a tiny little office space in

MY MIAMI 1992 - JANUARY (NEW YEAR, NEW DRAMA)

Coconut Grove. My Dad's an engineer, and my mom works from home as a customer serve representative.

My family always prioritized education, my dad always spoke about how a good education could bring anyone far in life. Which is why they registered Martin and me into one of the most highly ranked schools in the Grove: the Coconut Grove Academy. It was a traditional private school, with school uniforms, strict teachers, and very high school fees. My Mom and Dad put so much money into my brother and I's schooling, that they barely had any money left for us to move into a new house. I was so grateful for all my parents had done for me and hoped that one day they would be able to buy their dream house in the suburbs like they'd always wanted to.

My school life was quite decent, mainly because I went to the same school as my best friend (Meghan Benjaminson) and was a member of the most popular group in school. Meghan and I's parents knew each other before we were even born. When we initially met, Meghan and I were not the best of friends and highly disliked each other. Our parents thought that our relationship would get better over the years, but when it eventually didn't, they decided to take matters into their own hands. In the summer of going to grade four, our parents sent us to summer camp together and schemed for us to be roommates. They thought we were going to eat each other alive, but to everyone's we became good friends all the way till now.

MY MIAMI 1992 - JANUARY (NEW YEAR, NEW DRAMA)

"Okay kids, listen to Martin," Mom said as she put on her jacket.

"Let's hope we don't get drunk!" Dad laughed as he opened the door. I watched as my mom rolled her eyes behind his back. Mrs. Benjaminson kissed Meghan on the forehead and walked out the door followed by her husband. After all the good-byes and listen-to-Martin's, our parents had finally left. When Martin closed the door, he grinned at us slyly. Uh-oh! I had a feeling it was going to be a long night.

"Martin, we're going to watch TV" I announced stubbornly, "I want to watch the replay of the ball drop in Times Square."

Meghan and I were dying to watch it, but our parents wouldn't let us watch it live (for family quality time purposes).

"Yeah! Great idea!" Meghan agreed, as she walked towards the couch in front of the TV.

"No way!" Martin interjected, "It's twelve o'clock, way too late for you two."

"Oh please! We can sleep at whatever time we want," Meghan told him.

"Agreed," I chimed (even though I knew *I* wasn't).

"I'm in charge," Martin said proudly.

I stuck my tongue out at him, as he parked himself in front of the TV.

MY MIAMI 1992 - JANUARY (NEW YEAR, NEW DRAMA)

"Such a jerk," I muttered.

"I wish you guys had two TVs," Meghan said as we headed into the bathroom to brush our teeth. I stared at Meghan as she grabbed the brand-new toothbrush in the cabinet under the sink.

"What?" she asked as she ripped open the cardboard wrapper (Meghan hated being stared at, it made her insecure, but I personally thought that she had nothing to be insecure about). However, the reason I was staring at her toothbrush was because I had the best plan ever to get back at Martin.

"I have an idea…" I told her.

We washed ourselves up and went to my bedroom to wait for Martin to react to our ultimate prank. If you're wondering what our prank was, we put the smelly shampoo that I had received from one of my aunts for Christmas into Martin's toothbrush. It was going to be hilarious!

As we waited for Martin's reaction, Meghan asked me thoughtfully, "Have you thought of your new year's resolution yet?"

I sighed, it had honestly never really crossed my mind, I had my head so wrapped around Christmas, I barely had a chance to register that it was a new year.

"No, not yet, I'll probably have something figured out in the morning," I replied.

"Well, I'm going to be a vegetarian."

MY MIAMI 1992 - JANUARY (NEW YEAR, NEW DRAMA)

I nodded in agreement. Meghan was very fussy about what type of meat she ate. She hated burgers, hot dogs, drumsticks, and much more. The only type of meat she liked was the orange popcorn chicken that they served at the school cafeteria. So, going vegetarian for Meghan was going to be a piece of cake for her.

"Good luck," I told her, even though I knew she didn't need it.

We waited patiently for Martin to come upstairs and brush his teeth, but all he was doing was watching the replay of an American football game. I knew because I could hear the extra loud sounds of people screaming and yelling 'SCORE!' or 'BOO!' from the TV along with Martin's additional "sound effects".

We waited for so long that Meghan eventually ended up falling asleep on my bed instead of the sleeping bag I usually gave her when she slept over. Since my twin bed was way too small for the both of us, I decided to take the sacrifice and sleep in the uncomfortable sleeping bag.

While I waited, I began to read a brand-new book by my favourite author, Rayne Weaver. It was titled "The Weavers Save the Planet." A book about how Rayne and her family started a charity business to help their city Coral Springs open its first ever Recycling Depot in order to diminish the number of bottles being wasted. Rayne Weaver was such a huge inspiration to me, and one day I wanted to meet her. Ever

MY MIAMI 1992 - JANUARY (NEW YEAR, NEW DRAMA)

since I read her first novel I had been obsessed with reading, and one day aspired to be a writer. To be just like Rayne Weaver and aspire youngsters like me to have a relationship with God was my biggest dream.

I kept on reading the book, until I finally finished. As I was looking over the author's biography page, I noticed that Rayne Weaver's PO box address was provided alongside her information. I could send her letters! I reviewed the PO box address, realized that Rayne Weaver lived in Orlando, Florida. She must have moved towns, because according to her book she was born in Coral Springs.

Then, out of nowhere, an amazing idea popped into my head. I could write letters to Rayne Weaver - once a week! It was an amazing idea! There was so much I wanted to ask her and learn about her success! I quickly grabbed my notebook from my cupboard before I could forget my new goal for the year.

"What are you doing?" Meghan groaned as she rolled on the other side of her back (She probably had heard the loud noises of me fiercely scribbling onto my notebook).

"I found out what I want my new year's resolution to be!" I told her with enthusiasm.

"Okay then, good night," Meghan yawned without reflecting my energy.

MY MIAMI 1992 - JANUARY (NEW YEAR, NEW DRAMA)

I couldn't help myself as I squealed with utter delight, "I'm going to write a letter to Rayne Weaver every week, for the rest of the year!"

"Okay then, goodnight," Meghan repeated dryly, as she turned around, and covered her face with my blanket.

I decided to leave Meghan alone and wrote my very first letter to my personal icon Rayne Weaver.

Dear Rayne Weaver,

Hi! My name is Jennifer. I'm a great fan of yours and I absolutely LOVE your books. I just finished reading your best-selling book "The Weavers Save the Planet," and I absolutely love it! It's pretty cool to read about how close you were to your family... I wish I was as close to my sibling as you were, but my Martin can be really annoying and immature at times. I just wanted you to know that you're an amazing author!! I really would like to get to learn more about you, and I cannot wait for you to respond to this letter! Also, HAPPY NEW YEAR! I hope last year was a good year for you, and I hope that this year will be 10 times even better! Your BIGGEST FAN

Jennifer Chevrolet :)

I wanted to find an envelope and some stamps and put my letter outside in the mailbox that instant, but of course I couldn't because I knew that my mom would flip if she found out that I went outside this late at night. Miami was not the safest city, especially at night, for young girls like me. So, I let go of my

MY MIAMI 1992 - JANUARY (NEW YEAR, NEW DRAMA)

excitement and put the letter in my cupboard, said a little prayer that Rayne Weaver would see it and respond, then went to bed.

*****

I'm not exactly how much later, but Meghan and I were both woken up with a huge exclamation from Martin, "YUCK!" We giggled so hard our sides hurt. Martin had gotten his revenge! Seeing that Meghan was finally awake, I took the opportunity to explain my New Year's resolution to her.

"Good idea! If you're sending letters every week she will just have to respond," Meghan said.

"I hope so," I replied hopefully. Meghan was about to say something but was interrupted by Martin stomping into my bedroom and turning the lights on.

"I'm going to get you back," he said, pointing his index finger at us. Meghan and I laughed as he stormed back to his bedroom and angrily slammed the door. After the laughter over Martin's tantrum died down, we chatted a little bit more about our new year resolutions, and quickly went back to sleep (we were not sure when our parents would be back and didn't want them to find us awake that late at night).

*****

Meghan stayed over at our house for the rest of the day. We gossiped, played video

MY MIAMI 1992 - JANUARY (NEW YEAR, NEW DRAMA)

games, had snacks, and watched movies. It was an unproductive, but fun New Year's Day. School would be starting next week, so it was important that I got all the rest I could. I was also able to put my first letter to Rayne Weaver in the mailbox. It was the start of a New Year. 1991 was gone and passed, now it was time for 1992!

MY MIAMI 1992 - JANUARY (NEW YEAR, NEW DRAMA)

Thursday, January 2nd, 1992

My excitement and curiosity couldn't hold me back from checking the mailbox that morning. However, to my demise, the only letter I received was my school schedule. Not a response from Rayne Weaver. Plus, it was old mail because nobody had checked our mailbox in days. Lovely.

I knew that I shouldn't have been expecting a response the day after I sent out the letter, but my enthusiasm got the best of me. So, when I headed over to the mailbox that morning expecting a fresh new letter from my favourite author, but in turn received a school schedule - I was far from pleased.

Meghan was the only one who knew and understood how excited I was about my new year's resolution, so she gave me a call from her house to see if the response had arrived. She was such a good friend

"So? So? Did you get a reply?" she asked without even saying hello.

"Hi Meg! My day has been wonderful so far," I laughed.

"Whatever, did Rayne Weaver reply? Did she?"

"Meghan, I only put the letter in the mail yesterday."

"Well, I guess you're right, but-"

MY MIAMI 1992 - JANUARY (NEW YEAR, NEW DRAMA)

I heard some muffled voices in the background.

"Oh, sorry Jen! I wish I could talk more but my mom wants to take me out to buy my school uniform."

"Don't you already have like five sets?"

"My old ones are too small - well according to my mom they are."

"Wow! You're probably going to have 100 of sets of uniforms by the time you are done with school."

"And I lost my ribbon… again."

I laughed, said goodbye to Meghan, then sighed. It had always been funny to me how Meghan and I were the best of friends but lived completely different lives. You see, Meghan's family could afford to buy her how many school uniform sets she wanted. Mine could only afford to buy me two (one of which is my gym uniform).

I wandered out of my room and picked up my blue journal. Out of complete boredom, I started jotting down Meghan and I's most obvious differences.

JENNIFER VS MEGHAN

JENNIFER	MEGHAN
- Brunette	- Blonde
- Born Monday, February 26th, 1979	- Born Monday, February 12th, 1979

MY MIAMI 1992 - JANUARY (NEW YEAR, NEW DRAMA)

- Has one older sibling   - An only child

I peered at my list. I was unsatisfied. I had only written down the most basic things. I shut my notebook, laid down on my bed, and stared at my bedroom ceiling.

I sat up and looked at my room, it was boring, it was filled with my desk and chair, drawer, bed, closet, a blue lamp, a few print out photos (of friends and family), and two posters. I stared at the posters taped (we were renting our house, and my dad wouldn't let us pin stuff on our walls) on my white wall, one poster said, "Life is better when you dance" and another was one I had received as a Christmas gift "New Year, New Me."

I laughed to myself, it was a common understanding that "New Year, New Me" was a lie that people always said to make themselves feel better. For the first week of January everyone had a New Year's Resolution that they aim for but ending up giving up by the time February hits. Last year, my resolution was to read and be open to other books other than just Rayne Weaver books, but obviously I failed. Although I knew that there was no way I would become a "new" person in 1992, I wanted it to be a special year where I defeated all the odds and kept my New Year's Resolution. I then began to wonder… There had to be something new coming my way in 1992! What could it be?

New Year, New… What could I have finished the sentence with?

MY MIAMI 1992 - JANUARY (NEW YEAR, NEW DRAMA)

Friday, January 3rd, 1992

```
That afternoon I came back from a bike ride
around the neighborhood with my brother and
stopped by the mailbox to surprisingly see
a letter with no address on it. It was
definitely hand delivered. That was odd.
Especially since it normally takes about a
week for new mail to arrive.
```

Dear reader,

Thank you for the kind letter. I genuinely appreciate it! Let me tell you a little bit about myself. First my name is Rayne Benjaminson (as you probably already know). I'm currently 21 years old, and I'm pursuing a degree in education at the University of Tumbleson, and I'm in my third year! I cannot wait to graduate! In my spare time, I like to take long walks along campus pathways, write books, and volunteer as a substitute teacher at the Coconut Grove Academy! I hope you've learned something new about me! Thanks for reading my books!

- Rayne Benjaminson

```
"Wait what?" I exclaimed after I read the
letter almost four times (I was convinced
that I had read it wrong).
```

```
"Since when was she 21 years old and still
in university? Wait - she volunteers at my
school? And why does she have the same last
name as Meghan?" I exclaimed when I showed
my mom the letter. "And why did I receive a
reply so fast? She lives in Orlando! It
should have taken at least a week!"
```

MY MIAMI 1992 - JANUARY (NEW YEAR, NEW DRAMA)

"Woah! Slow your horses, sweetie," my mom teased.

"This letter just confuses me," I groaned in frustration.

"Maybe, you could talk to Meghan about her last name, maybe she knows; but remember, people can have the same last names and not be related."

"And this letter is not in handwriting; it's in a printed font," My Dad chuckled, as he peered over my shoulder.

"Yeah, I'm pretty sure this letter is sent to everyone that sends this author of yours a letter," My Mom laughed along.

I didn't like how my own parents seemed to be amused by my misfortune. This was my New Year's resolution, and I was serious about it. I wanted to be taken seriously.

"I'm calling Meghan," I said. I didn't want any help from my mom and dad if all they were going to do was laugh about it. I headed up to my room and closed the door.

The most critical question that I needed to an answer to was how in the world did Meghan and Rayne Weaver end up having the same last name. I knew that it could possibly just be a coincidence… you never know. I called Meghan (Meghan has her own personal number), but to my surprise Mrs. B answered instead.

"Hello?" She greeted me.

MY MIAMI 1992 - JANUARY (NEW YEAR, NEW DRAMA)

"Hi Mrs. B it's me, Jennifer," I replied. I should have spoken to Mrs. B first, but I felt like speaking with Meghan at that moment.

Mrs. B let out a huge sigh and said, "Okay, but only for five minutes, she's working on her book report."

I slapped my forehead. I had completely forgotten about the book report that was due next week (it was worth 15% of our grade). I decided to hide that fact from Mrs. B because I didn't want her to rat me out to my parents. My parents – especially my dad – were very strict about my grades and I didn't want them to be on my case about it. Overhearing the way my dad chased Martin around certainly did not make me want any of that parental attention. I made a mental note to complete the assignment before school resumed.

Mrs. B called Meghan over; we greeted each other quickly, and I gave her the somewhat good news.

"She replied to my letter," I told her.

"Huh?" Meghan questioned in confusion.

"Rayne Weaver!" I prompted her aggressively. Meghan should have understood what I meant. It was all I had spoken about since New Year's. How could she forget this quickly?

"Geez! My ears. You don't have to yell," Meghan scoffed.

MY MIAMI 1992 - JANUARY (NEW YEAR, NEW DRAMA)

"Sorry," I apologized, even though I technically wasn't yelling.

"It's super cool that she replied to your letter! And so fast too!" she congratulated, "Read it to me."

"She didn't *actually* reply to my letter. The letter I received was just a copy of the one she sends to everyone who sends mail."

"Okay. Can you still read it to me though?"

"Sure."

I read the letter and Meghan listened quietly.

"I'm lost," Meghan said when I finished.

"Why does she have the same last name as you?" I asked.

"I don't know," Meghan responded, "And why did you get a reply so fast? The mail normally takes a week to deliver."

"I also noticed that there wasn't an address on the envelope. It must have been hand-delivered."

"Maybe she lives nearby?"

"Hmm... Maybe."

"Or maybe-" Meghan began, but she was interrupted by a voice in the background.

MY MIAMI 1992 - JANUARY (NEW YEAR, NEW DRAMA)

I immediately knew it was her mom - Mrs. B. Mrs. Benjaminson was probably one of the most overprotective moms I had ever seen. However, to a certain degree, it did make sense because Meghan was an only child, with many allergies, and asthma. I loved Mrs. B, she was like a second mother to me, but I felt that she needed to ease up a little. It always felt as though Meghan was a bird in a cage. My mom was ten times definitely more laid back and chill than Mrs. B, but I knew that she always meant well. I smiled. I had found another comparison to add to my list!

"Sorry Jennifer, Meghan has to go work on her book report now…," Mrs. B told me, after what felt like hours of squabbling between mother and daughter.

It had always surprised me how Meghan could get away with arguing with her mom, but if I even tried to "talk back" to mine I would be grounded. Wow! Another point for my list!

"Okay, but Mrs. B?"

"Yes, sweetheart?"

"Are you related to anyone named Rayne Benjaminson?" I asked.

"Umm… maybe you should ask my husband. He should know, after all, that would be on his side of the family. He's at work now… Should I give you his work number?"

"Yes please, but I'd rather not have his direct work phone number; maybe his

MY MIAMI 1992 - JANUARY (NEW YEAR, NEW DRAMA)

secretary's number so I could leave him a message instead?"

Mrs. B gave me Mr. Benjaminson's secretary's number and we hung up. I called her and left a message requesting Mr. B. to call me back.

Mr. Benjaminson was the owner of a successful real estate company in Westchester and was quite a busy man. "He's *always* working," Meghan would complain to me. Mr. B was always on the run and was not the type to be pleased when interrupted from his work. Mr. B is probably the coolest guy ever when he's not working. I knew that from experience.

One time, when my parents went to Orlando for a week to celebrate their 18th anniversary (I was about nine years old at that time) while Martin and I stayed with the Benjaminsons. One day, Mrs. B went to the grocery store with Martin and was supposed to come back before Mr. B had to go to work. Unfortunately, but expectedly (since we lived in Miami), she got caught up in traffic. So, because Meghan and I were too young to be home alone, Mr. B had no choice but to take us to his office.

We waited forever in what was probably the most boring lobby in the world. It consisted of one TV which was only playing the local news, some chairs, a half-empty vending machine, and a rude secretary who ignored us when we asked to change the channel.

MY MIAMI 1992 - JANUARY (NEW YEAR, NEW DRAMA)

So, we decided to innocently go inside Mr. B's office (without knocking) to ask for coins for the vending machine and a remote for the TV. Mr. B then angrily threw a bunch of coins at us and scolded us, "Get out of my office! Can't you see I'm busy?!". Of course, being nine-year-olds, we left the room in tears. Being overcome by guilt, Mr. B later apologized over a dozen times and earned our forgiveness with ice cream.

I was dying to find out if Meghan was truly related to my favourite author, but I definitely was not willing to go through an angry Mr. B to do it.

MY MIAMI 1992 – JANUARY (NEW YEAR, NEW DRAMA)

Saturday, January 4th, 1992

Dear Rayne Weaver,

I know this is the second letter that I am sending you, but this time, could you please send me a REAL reply to that letter I sent you on January 1st? This is not to say that the other letter was fake, but it seems as if that letter was a generic one for responding to fan mail. I also noticed that it has the wrong information according to your most recent autobiography. Maybe you could consider creating an updated fan letter, so it's current. That would keep your fans informed of your latest achievements.

Today I found out that you could be related to one of my friends. Perhaps you know her? Meghan Benjaminson? She claims to have never met you, but maybe you've heard of her? Her Dad's name is Mr. Anderson Benjaminson (I like to call him Mr. B, it has a nice ring to it). Since I received your reply so fast, I believe that you might live in MIAMI!! I live in Miami too! Maybe I can meet you one day! FINGERS CROSSED! PLEASE RESPOND!!

Jennifer Chevrolet

```
That morning, I surprisingly woke up early,
went downstairs for breakfast, and met my
dad and Mr. B chatting about the recent
football game over coffee (All the boys in
my house and Mr. B, my dad were huge
football fans).

"Yes," Mr. B. said when I asked him about
his relation to Rayne Weaver, "Rayne is my
younger  sister,  the  youngest  in  the
family."
```

MY MIAMI 1992 - JANUARY (NEW YEAR, NEW DRAMA)

"Wow, that's so cool!" I beamed. It felt almost impossible to hold all my excitement in.

"Yes, it is," he chuckled, "We haven't spoken in a while, but I know that last time we spoke she said she was moving to Miami. Her husband works in the real estate market as well."

"Has Meghan met her?"

"Not really, she came to Meghan's baby shower, but she was way too young to remember."

"I can't believe Meghan is related to a celebrity."

"Well, I wouldn't say celebrity, but it's cool that you see her that way. I'm always happy to see that my little sister has many fans," said Mr. B.

My Dad, who seemed to be completely drained out of the situation, tapped my shoulder and said, "Don't you have some homework to do?" I nodded.

I wanted to continue my conversation with Mr. B to find out more, but I knew that my dad's word was final. It was time for homework. Great.

Once I got back into my room, I groaned as I stared at my desk which had two double-sided sheets of questions about the book we were supposed to read over the winter break. Ms. Sanicharan (my English teacher) was probably one of the best teachers at

MY MIAMI 1992 - JANUARY (NEW YEAR, NEW DRAMA)

CGA (Coconut Grove Academy), but I did not enjoy the fact that she gave us homework over the holidays. I mean – what was the point of a break if we got homework?

The part that I disliked the most about the homework was that I couldn't choose which story to write my book report on. Each student was assigned a different fictional book, mine was "The Sunflower's Passion", written by a man named Rick Finkle (weird name, right?!).

It was a beautiful inspirational story, but not fun to read at all, especially since I was obligated to read it when I just wanted to relax and enjoy my holidays.

Obviously, I preferred to do my book study to a book by Rayne Weaver. Most of her books were real stories from her childhood and I preferred books that were not only realistic but also relatable.

However, because I craved academic validation, I completed the assignment as if I loved it. I reread my work, fixed up a few mistakes, and smiled in satisfaction when I felt it was perfect.

With my book report finished it was finally official. Jennifer Chevrolet was ready for school.

MY MIAMI 1992 - JANUARY (NEW YEAR, NEW DRAMA)

Sunday, January 5th, 1992

Dear reader,

Thank you for your kind letter. I truly appreciate it, and I'm glad that my books were able to inspire you enough that you wrote a letter to me...

"Argh!" I groaned.

It was a hot sunny Sunday in the Grove, Miami, Florida. I had promised Meghan that the next time I received a letter from Rayne Weaver, I'd open it with her. So, after church service (our families have been attending the same church for years) Meghan asked me to come over so we could do it together.

I probably was at the Benjaminson family household every week. It was practically a second home. The house was *huge*! It had five bedrooms (some of which they didn't even use), two offices, two dining room spaces, an outdoor pool, and so much more. Meghan had a room that every girl our age would die for. It had a queen-sized bed (with almost a dozen pillows), a vanity, a dresser, a walk-in closet, and get this - a balcony! You'd think her room was the master bedroom. Meghan's room was entirely decorated by her mom and therefore was very pink and girly. She hated how pink it was. Meghan was a certified tomboy.

Personally, if my room had looked anything near Meghan's I would never want to leave. Yes, it definitely was a lot of pink, but it was still such a nice room. Meghan was

MY MIAMI 1992 - JANUARY (NEW YEAR, NEW DRAMA)

so lucky that her family was able to afford to get her such nice stuff like a perfectly decorated room. If I was her, I would have been grateful.

Meghan and I read the letter, then I told her about the conversation I had with Mr. B.

"What!" she gasped. "I'm related to an author. How come he didn't tell me?"

A spark of envy flared in me. Meghan had everything. The feeling of being envious of my best friend disgusted me, but I couldn't help it.

"Hello? Earth to Jen?" Meghan teased with a giggle.

"Oh, sorry Meg! I was daydreaming," I laughed. "I can't believe you're related to Rayne Weaver."

"Yeah, and sorry about your letter," she said.

"I guess Benjaminson was her last name before she got married - I wonder if your dad attended her wedding."

"He probably did, why don't we ask him," Meghan offered, grabbing my hand.

Meghan dragged me into Mr. B's home office and barged in without knocking. I was in awe that Mr. B would tolerate such a thing, but then again, this was "home", not the official workplace in Westchester.

MY MIAMI 1992 - JANUARY (NEW YEAR, NEW DRAMA)

We walked into Mr. B's office and Meghan let him know that I still had a few more questions about Rayne Weaver that I wanted to ask.

As I was bombarding Mr. B with questions, he admitted that he wasn't close to his sister and that for the most part of growing up, they didn't really get along. To help out, he let us know that Rayne was closer to his other sibling, Phil. Mr. B then went on to recite to us stories of how his younger sister and older brother always got into a lot of mischief together. He also told us that he was more of a loner and quite a bookworm, always quietly reading by himself.

He gave us his brother Phil's number so we could give him a phone call. As we were heading upstairs, I asked Meghan (probably for the 100th time), "Are you sure you don't remember her from when you were a baby?"

In response Meghan gave me a strong eye roll. I got the message. Who remembers anyone from when they were babies?

"How many times do I need to tell you? I don't know her. I don't remember her! How can a one-week-old baby even do that? Is that even possible?" Meghan whispered in frustration.

Meghan had always had a quick temper.

"Would you like to call your uncle?" I inquired, hoping to shift the

MY MIAMI 1992 - JANUARY (NEW YEAR, NEW DRAMA)

conversation's focus before we had an argument.

"Nah… Maybe another day, I have a better idea," Meghan replied.

She looked under her pillow and found two pieces of gum. Meghan hid candy all over her room. Her mom was very particular and cautious about not indulging in candy. She'd go insane if she found out Meghan ate all that junk daily. For one thing, she was concerned about Meghan's health and not getting obese or cavities.

"Why don't you want to call your uncle?" I asked as I popped a piece of gum in my mouth.

"He's a freak! The last time he called to say hello for my ninth birthday, he said that he wouldn't attend my birthday party then because he was afraid of balloons and circuses!" she chuckled, but her tone was solemn.

"Balloons and circuses?" I exclaimed in laughter.

"I understand the circus, clowns are so creepy, but not balloons," Meghan said, "But listen, here's my idea. We can go find out where Rayne Weaver lives, by ourselves."

"What? Do you know how big Miami is? We would be looking for days," I pointed out. "Plus, why would we go looking for her when we could just ask your dad for her address?"

MY MIAMI 1992 - JANUARY (NEW YEAR, NEW DRAMA)

"Do you want to find her or not?" Meghan challenged me. I nodded with uncertainty.

I wanted to meet Rayne Weaver face to face. Since she apparently was not in the habit of replying to her fan mail, meeting her in person was going to have to be the way to go. I had so many questions to ask her, and a face-to-face encounter was just what I needed. But I wasn't willing to get lost in such a huge city just do it, and I told Meghan as much.

It would be much safer to start our research with Meghan's uncle. I assumed they'd know exactly where Rayne lived, saving us the trouble of attempting to find her ourselves. Miami was such a large metropolis, and it could easily "consume" two twelve-year-old's who didn't know where to look.

"Let's call your uncle," I said to Meghan. "It's safer that way".

"Fine. But let me warn you! He's nuts!" Meghan warned, as she directed herself towards her phone. "I mean nuts."

Meghan picked up her phone and dialed in her uncle's phone number. She had to call twice before he picked up.

"Sorry! I thought you were the secret agency trying to take me out of the farmer business," he said instantly.

Meghan had informed me before she called that Phil lived in Alabama and spoke with a southern American accent. It sounded so natural, but he was obviously faking it. The Benjaminsons (Rayne, Mr. B, and Phil) grew up in Coral Gables. And I knew of no one in Florida who spoke with a southern accent.

Meghan gave me the "I told you so!" look, but I ignored her and continued to listen to him. He seemed a little wacky, but I liked him.

"Unless you two are trying to take me out of the farming business… How can I help y'all?" he asked.

"Hi Uncle Phil, it's me, your niece Meghan," Meghan told him.

"Meghan the pig? Or Meghan the kid? Did y'all, know I do happen to have a pig named Meghan. I named that cute little thing after my cute 'n little niece Meghan was born."

I couldn't help letting out a little giggle as Meghan rolled her eyes.

"It's me, Meghan, your niece!" she answered sharply. She was clearly irritated that her uncle had named a pig after her.

"Ouch! I just got this hearing aid mended three days ago after my pet rooster crowed right beside my ear," he grumbled. Meghan at gestured me to take the floor.

"Hello, I'm Jennifer, Meghan's best friend," I introduced myself. Meghan nodded.

MY MIAMI 1992 - JANUARY (NEW YEAR, NEW DRAMA)

We waited for a response, then suddenly the line went dead. Great.

So much for Uncle Phil!

MY MIAMI 1992 - JANUARY (NEW YEAR, NEW DRAMA)

Monday, January 6th, 1992

I awoke that morning, ecstatic since it was a public holiday, the Epiphany, which meant no school. It allowed me to have more time for Rayne Weaver research before school resumed the next day.

I resolved to be productive. I got up early, made myself pancakes, did some housework, and wrote another letter to Rayne Weaver.

Dear Rayne Weaver,

It's me, Jennifer again. I know I've been sending you a lot of letters recently. I'm not trying to annoy you or waste your time. I just really want you to know that I am genuinely a huge fan of your work! I would really appreciate it if you responded to my letter. Please!

Jennifer Chevrolet

I re-read my letter and grinned with contentment. Rayne Weaver would just *have* to glance at it, considering how brief it was. I eagerly placed it into our mailbox.

It was now time to head to Meghan's. I was beginning to consider taking Meghan's Miami search suggestion, but first I wanted to see if we could get a direct address from Mr. B.

I was on my way to the garage to retrieve my bike when my mom stopped me. What did she want? I had already completed all my chores for the day (which is what I had to do before I left the house)!

MY MIAMI 1992 - JANUARY (NEW YEAR, NEW DRAMA)

"Where are you going, miss?" she asked.

"I'm heading over to Meghan's," I explained.

"Weren't you at her place yesterday?" my mother asked.

"Yeah... What's the big deal?"

She raised her eyebrow.

"You've been obsessed with going over to the Benjaminsons' these past few days, that you haven't been spending valuable time with your family," my mother complained. "Today we are having an FBT!"

"FBT?" I repeated.

"Family Bonding Time," she explained, "It's so sad you can't even remember. It's been so long since we've done it."

I tried to get out of whatever the FBT thing was, but I couldn't. We watched a Disney film about a princess (Beauty and the Beast). I feigned to dislike the film in order to make my mom feel bad for denying me the opportunity to go over to Meghan's house.

I contacted Meghan after the movie to ask if I could still come over, but she had to decline since her mom said it was time for Meghan to prepare for school. It was as if both of our moms had made a plan that we did not see each other that day. Parents!

MY MIAMI 1992 - JANUARY (NEW YEAR, NEW DRAMA)

I was going to hang up from the call until Meghan abruptly said - "New student alert!"

"Huh?"

"You heard me," Meghan laughed loudly

"Really? Wait. Who?"

"Some girl named Talia," Meghan said in a sly voice.

"Okay? What's so special about her?" I asked. Why was Meghan acting so suspicious? What was going on?

"Her last name..." Meghan said slowly.

"What's her last name?" I asked, my patience dwindling.

"Weaver!" Meghan announced finally. "Talia Weaver... There's no way that's just a coincidence."

Weaver... Weaver... Rayne Weaver... Talia Weaver! Oh, my goodness. Was it possible? Could they be related? My pulse raced with ecstasy. I was at a complete loss for words.

I was going to ask more questions, but Meghan quickly ended the call with, "M'kay, got to go now! Bye!".

Classic Meghan. Always leaving you in suspense. I couldn't wait until school tomorrow to find out more about this Talia Weaver girl.

MY MIAMI 1992 - JANUARY (NEW YEAR, NEW DRAMA)

You may be wondering right now why I am so obsessed with discovering more about Rayne Weaver. Well, a few weeks ago, I had this amazing idea to write a magazine piece about her. I hadn't decided on all the specifics yet, but I wanted to write a biographical essay about her in one of Florida's most popular magazines, Project Authors.

The Project Authors magazine held a yearly challenge in which students aged 13 to 16 wrote a biography about an author of their choosing. The magazine editors would then choose a winner, and the winner's biographical article would be published in the magazine.

The winner would also earn a $10,000 award. I really wanted to use that money to help my family move out of our old condominium complex and buy a new house in the suburbs. My parents constantly talked about trying to buy a new house, but they were never able to do it because of funds they put into Martin's and I's education and other things. My parents made several sacrifices to ensure my brother and I's success in life, and I owed it to them to earn the money and deliver it to them.

Even though I was only twelve years old, I would be turning thirteen in February, so I could gather all my research and prepare my essay ahead of time.

Meghan knew about my research on Rayne Weaver, but she wasn't aware of the real reason I wanted to do it. It's not that I didn't trust Meghan (I did, most of the

MY MIAMI 1992 - JANUARY (NEW YEAR, NEW DRAMA)

time), it's just that I didn't want to tell her. Or anyone for that matter. It was my little secret.

*****

A few hours after Meghan's news, I received a phone call from someone I didn't necessarily feel like talking to. Ever.

In order to understand why I didn't find this phone call amusing; you have to understand my friend group.

It's known as "The 'It' Clique". Which consisted of me, Meghan Benjaminson, Charlotte Riehl, Rosalyn Smith, Emerald Humphrey, and Skye Murray (the one I received a phone call from). Meghan Benjaminson, my best friend, was the head of the It Clique.

Being Meghan's childhood best friend, I was automatically granted a spot in the It Clique. However, I wasn't really friends with any of the girls besides Meghan. In fact, if it wasn't for Meghan, I probably would have been the last person allowed to join. Some of the girls didn't even want me around (especially Skye), but since I was Meghan's best friend there was nothing they could really do about it.

Meghan was by far the most popular girl in our grade and was the one who created the group. If the It Clique were a monarchy, Meghan would be the reigning queen, Skye would be her chief advisor, and the others would be the members of council. All the

MY MIAMI 1992 - JANUARY (NEW YEAR, NEW DRAMA)

pupils served as our subjects. The school practically served as our royal residence.

It was exciting to be a member of the It Clique, but I always ended up feeling like an outsider. I had always felt as though no one there actually liked me. So, you could imagine my surprise when I receive a call from the one and only Skye Murray (who was always the loudest about not liking me).

"Hey Jenny," she greeted when I picked up.

Skye was the only person on earth who called me "Jenny" - and she was well aware that I disliked it. The sound of her voice always felt calm and expressionless, yet she always used it to spread lies, criticism, and almost any negative thing you can think of. She had one of the most poisonous personalities I had ever seen. I had no idea how Meghan was good friends with her.

"Hi Skye," I took a deep breath and exhaled, "How can I help you?"

"Just so you that you recognize me tomorrow, I just wanted you to know that I dyed my hair blonde, just like Meghan's!" she bragged, "I got it from that fancy hair salon where Meghan gets her hair trimmed. How about that?"

I sighed and rolled my eyes. Skye was the most self-centered individual on the earth. She'd always wanted to get close to Meghan (just as I was), but for the wrong reasons. Skye was determined to destabilize the monarchy and dethrone Meghan at school. And the only way she could do that was by replacing me as Meghan's best friend. It was so obvious that Skye's true intentions with Meghan were to replace her. It felt as though no one understood that but me.

"That's great, Skye," I said in a fake cheery voice.

"I know, right? I've been thinking about getting it permed. What do you think?"

"Skye, was there an important reason why you called me?" I asked, annoyed. I was starting to consider just hanging up.

"Oh, yeah! So, Meghan told me that she talked to her dad about the new girl Talia, and she's this lady Rayne Weaver's daughter apparently," Skye laughed, "Who's Rayne Weaver anyway?"

I was shocked. How come Skye was receiving this information before me? W

"Wait - when did she tell you this?" I asked.

"Uh - like this morning? She called me when she woke up."

I let Skye talk about her amazing life for a few more moments while I puzzledly stared at my wall. Why hadn't Meghan told me all the details when we were on the phone? She obviously knew that I would want and need to know that, so why wouldn't she tell me?

Skye and I were just wrapping up our one-sided conversation when she said, "Don't

MY MIAMI 1992 - JANUARY (NEW YEAR, NEW DRAMA)

tell Meghan I told you about the new girl thing."

"Why?"

"I don't know, I don't think she wanted me to tell you, or something. She was so secretive about it."

Meghan had a lot of explaining to do…

MY MIAMI 1992 - JANUARY (NEW YEAR, NEW DRAMA)

Tuesday, January 7th, 1992

It was my first day back at school after the holidays, and I couldn't wait to meet Talia. I went to Meghan's house incredibly early to get more information from her since she hadn't given me any so far. I left a letter for my dad, informing him that I would be home in time for him to drop me off at school.

Alongside requesting more information, I was also going to confront Meghan on the fact that she didn't tell me that Talia was *her* cousin. It didn't make any sense to me why she told Skye instead of me. Skye wasn't even involved in my research in any way. One part of me wanted to believe that Skye was just lying, but the other knew she wasn't. That was probably one of the first times Skye wasn't spreading lies.

I got to Meghan's house and rang the doorbell twice.

"I'm coming!" I heard Meghan groan through the door, "Who visits people at 7:00 o'clock in the morning?"

I felt bad for coming so early in the morning, but technically it was her fault. It could have been avoided if she had just told me everything I needed to know about the new girl.

"Jen?" Meghan rubbed her eyes, looked at me up and down, then glanced at the watch on her wrist, "It's 7:16 A.M.! Don't we have school? You didn't even tell me you were coming over."

MY MIAMI 1992 - JANUARY (NEW YEAR, NEW DRAMA)

"I know, and I'm sorry. I just really need you to tell me more about the new girl," I pled.

Meghan stared at me for what seemed like forever, then said, "No, nothing besides the fact that her name is Talia Weaver."

"You sure?"

"Yes, I am sure Jennifer," Meghan said, rolling her eyes.

"Okay but Skye called me yesterday and said-"

"Look Jennifer, can you just let it go? I don't know anything. Isn't that enough for you?" she snapped.

Liar. Meghan had just lied straight to my face. She was supposed to be my best friend. How could she do that? I felt my body tighten in anger.

Meghan held out her hand toward the door, and I felt a twinge on the inside. Was Meghan mad at me?

"Wait - Meghan, are you mad at me?"

"No, just not in a good mood right now. Bye."

I left her house without saying a word. Suddenly I started having the feeling that Meghan and I were going to go through a friendship hurdle. I walked back home feeling sick.

MY MIAMI 1992 - JANUARY (NEW YEAR, NEW DRAMA)

My Dad was a little upset at me for going to Meghan's house so early, but luckily it had no impact on our ability to get to school on time.

It was the first day back to school after the holidays and deciding whether I was eager or tense about it day was difficult. I was eager to meet Talia, but nervous to deal with Meghan and I being in a weird spot. Meghan's displeasure with you was not good news.

I walked into the school courtyard to see the It Clique all huddled around each other in one big circle. As I walked towards them, interested in discovering what they were discussing, I noticed that they immediately stopped talking.

"Hey guys! What are you talking about?" I asked curiously.

"Nothing," Meghan said, jerking her head towards my direction, she quickly eyed all the girls, "Check out the new girl."

It was easy to spot who Talia was. She wasn't wearing her school uniform, so she really stood out.

She was sitting quietly on a bench a couple of meters away from us, drawing on a notepad and listening to music on her Walkman.

"Should we go talk to her?" I asked with enthusiasm.

MY MIAMI 1992 - JANUARY (NEW YEAR, NEW DRAMA)

"I mean - *you* can if you want to," Skye told me with a thick tone in her voice. That was how she always was with me.

"Nah - I also want to see what she's like," Meghan interjected, "For all we know she could make a good addition to the It Clique."

"Do we really need new members though?" Skye whispered under her breath.

"Yes, we do," I replied slyly, turning around to look at her. She stuck her tongue out at me, while I grinned.

I ran ahead of the group so I could be the first one to meet the "yet-to-be-confirmed" child of Rayne Weaver in person.

"Hi!" I greeted as I walked up to her, "Are you new here?"

"What does it look like?" she said, looking me up and down.

Okay, rude. She didn't even know me yet was already giving me attitude.

"Oh yeah, sorry, just a rhetorical question" I laughed ignoring her rudeness.

I was tempted to ask her about Rayne Weaver, but I knew that it would be weird to be getting all up in her business when we had just met.

"Hey," Meghan said when she and girls came over, "Talia, right?"

MY MIAMI 1992 - JANUARY (NEW YEAR, NEW DRAMA)

"In the flesh," she responded without looking up from her drawing.

Meghan snarked, "Nice outfit."

Talia finally looked up and scanned each one of us, one after the other.

"Let me guess, you're the popular girl group, and she's the queen bee?" Talia laughed while pointing at Meghan.

"Don't you ever call me that ever again," Meghan warned her sharply.

Then Meghan looked at me with a shrug, then back at the It Clique. "Well," she said to Talia, "If you want to hang out with us, you're welcome to ... once you change your attitude."

"I love your drawing, by the way," I said to change the mood. It was starting to feel tense.

"Meh - It's alright," Skye said out of nowhere. I shot her a dirty look.

"It's impressive. You should join the art club," Meghan said, then glared at Skye. I grinned, having Meghan on your side was undoubtedly the best feeling ever. Take that Skye!

Before Talia could respond, the bell rang, and we all scrambled to rush to our classrooms. Emerald had warned Talia that she better get to class quickly, and quite literally did. Without even saying goodbye, she picked up her things and left.

MY MIAMI 1992 - JANUARY (NEW YEAR, NEW DRAMA)

I walked into the classroom and handed in my completed book report.

"This looks great, Jennifer! Keep up the good work!" Ms. Sanicharan said when I placed my paper on her desk.

"Thanks!" I gave her a smile.

I was ecstatic that Ms. Sanicharan was pleased with me. My parents were quite strict about grades, so I made it a point to obtain at least an A- on every assignment and test.

I took my seat, expecting it to be a usual boring English class, until Talia walked into the classroom.

I was very intrigued by Talia, not only because she was related to my favourite author, but also because of how presented herself. She always carried a serious facial expression on her face and had the best posture I had ever seen. She had deep hazel-coloured eyes, a few brown freckles on her cheekbones, curly brown hair in a French braid, and caramel brown skin. She wore light blue jeans, an orange pullover, and white sneakers - instead of the school uniform. She stood behind Mrs. Sanicharan in front of the classroom, with her hands in her pockets.

You couldn't tell if Talia was pleased or displeased, amused or annoyed, or if she was insecure or confident. Her facial expressions and body language communicated nothing. It was fascinating that she was

MY MIAMI 1992 - JANUARY (NEW YEAR, NEW DRAMA)

able to conceal all her emotions in such a way.

"Class?" Mrs. Sanicharan said interrupting my thoughts. She placed one hand on Talia's shoulder, "This is Talia Weaver. She will be joining us for the rest of the school year. Please make her feel welcomed."

Talia didn't react, she just stood there and provided zero eye contact with anyone.

"Would you like to introduce yourself, Talia?" Ms. S. asked kindly.

"No thanks," Talia responded blankly.

It was obvious Mrs. S. took Talia's response as a surprise, so instead she asked us to ask Talia some questions about herself.

"Where did you move from?" a girl named Carolyn asked (an old friend of mine).

"Orlando," Talia answered. By the way she responded, I could tell she didn't want to be asked all these questions about her life.

"Do you have any siblings?" another student asked.

"Yeah."

Talia was being very vague with her answers. It was a little bit irritating, since we were all, as a class, trying to get to know her.

MY MIAMI 1992 - JANUARY (NEW YEAR, NEW DRAMA)

I slowly raised up my hand.

"What do your parents do for work?" I asked after a quick hesitation, "Why did you move here?"

"My dad's a teacher," Talia said staring her deep brown eyes into the depth of my soul, "I moved here cause why not?"

I gave up. It was clear that Talia did not want to address the fact that her mom was an author.

Talia sat a few columns away from me. Throughout the class, she never raised her hand or contributed to discussions; but whenever she was called upon, she always had the right answer.

*****

At lunch I rushed to the It Clique table to sit beside Meghan before Skye had a chance to steal my spot (which she did quite often).

"Is Talia in any of your classes?" Meghan asked when I sat down.

"She's in my gym class," Charlotte contributed.

"Yeah, she is in my English, math, and history class," I said.

I scanned the lunchroom to see Talia and potentially invite her to our table, but there was no sign of her.

MY MIAMI 1992 - JANUARY (NEW YEAR, NEW DRAMA)

"When you find her, go ahead, and welcome her to our table," Meghan said practically reading my mind.

I cringed internally. Why did it feel as if I needed Meghan's permission before doing anything?

"Is she your cousin?" I asked as I bit into my sandwich.

"Didn't we already talk about this? I said I don't know," Meghan said as she fiddled with her fork, "Don't really care right now either".

"That girl Talia has a real attitude problem," Skye complained as she walked over and placed her lunch tray on the table. "I saw her in the hallway and waved, she didn't even wave back."

"Reminds me of someone," I said just to make her shut up, "Look, Meghan, I don't know why you keep saying you don't know if Talia is your cousin, because Skye told me is yesterday."

Meghan glared at Skye, who looked away and shrunk into her seat. Then Meghan glared back at me, placed her metal fork harshly on the table and said, "Okay, will you just give this Rayne Weaver thing a break? It's all you ever talk about these days."

"But - It's my new year's resolution," I said quietly.

Everything in me wanted to tell Meghan about the Author's Project challenge, but I couldn't - at least not in front of Skye or anyone in the It Clique.

"I know, it's getting ridiculous."

Feeling the coldness in the air, Rosalyn quickly changed the subject. "Hey, did you guys hear about Mr. Franklin giving us a science pop quiz tomorrow? I overheard him in the teachers' lunchroom..."

I felt that sick feeling I had felt in the morning for the second time that day. My friendship with Meghan was getting rocky.

MY MIAMI 1992 - JANUARY (NEW YEAR, NEW DRAMA)

Wednesday, January 8th, 1992

I woke up that morning feeling hot and comfortable in my blanket. I was sweating. I only sweated after gym class or after being outside for a long time, not in my sleep! Was the air conditioner broken?

It was usually hot in Miami, but it was definitely not enough to make you sweat in your sleep. I rubbed my eyes with my sweaty fingers (I know, gross), and checked my clock; 9:38 A.M. I was late for school. Uh-oh.

"Mooom!!" I called as I quickly slipped out of bed and grabbed my slippers, "I'm late!"

I groaned as I heard my mom's steps, slowly walking towards my room. Why wasn't she in a rush?

I dashed into the bathroom.

"Mom? Is the car still here? I need to get to school, I have a science quiz!"

My mom finally reached the bathroom as I was swiftly brushing my teeth.

"What are you doing?" she asked.

"Can you turn up the air conditioner? It's so hot in here," I asked, ignoring her questions.

My Mom grabbed my shoulders, turning my body towards her.

MY MIAMI 1992 - JANUARY (NEW YEAR, NEW DRAMA)

"It's 91 degrees outside, school is closed," she said slowly, "Mark my words. Go... Back... To... Sleep."

I went back to my room feeling gleeful and downcast at the same time. Happy that I had more time to study for my science quiz, and sad that I would be missing a day to get to know Talia better and perhaps resolve my conflict with Meghan.

I decided to call her so we could resolve our little dispute, but she seemed more interested in celebrity gossip.

"Jelanie Simmons and Gordon Tamsen are getting married! I wonder what the wedding will be like. It will probably be fancy, with white and gold balloons, a beautiful gown for the bride, a tight suit for the groom, a huge cake, and -".

"Don't you want to talk about something else?" I interrupted her.

"No... Not really, why?" Meghan said in a surprised tone.

"Umm... *Hello*? Talia, we just met her, and I know she's your cousin. Skye told me. Which means she's related to you. Doesn't that sound interesting to you?" I complained.

"Not really; I mean like, what are we going to do about it? Invite ourselves over to her house just to meet her mom?" Meghan muttered.

MY MIAMI 1992 - JANUARY (NEW YEAR, NEW DRAMA)

What was her issue? Why did she have to be such a grouch?

I promised Meghan I'd call her back, but I never did. She didn't seem to care if I did anyways, so I decided, neither did I.

I thought about telling her about the Authors Project challenge, so she'd have more sympathy… No, the challenge was to be going to between me, myself, and I. Sorry Meghan!

MY MIAMI 1992 - JANUARY (NEW YEAR, NEW DRAMA)

Thursday, January 9th, 1992

I was soaked - not because I had "accidentally" drowned myself in water or entered the shower with my clothes on (that would be stupid), but because I was sweating heavily once more. It was 84 degrees outdoors, and I thought I was going to melt. Nonetheless, we still had to go to school because the temperatures had not yet reached 90 degrees (which was the threshold at which schools were closed).

No, I wasn't complaining. I'd lived in Miami my entire life, and I'd be the first to say that we were pampered with our weather. I was used to the daily hot weather, but the humidity got to me that day.

Or maybe it wasn't the humidity, but the mounting tension between Meghan and I, and the realization that we were on the verge of a major quarrel that might jeopardize our friendship. It may also have been the anxiousness that drove thoughts of Skye organizing a mission to strike high into the sky (see what I did there?) to push me to the brink of a nervous breakdown.

"Oh hey, Jenny," Skye waved at me, when I walked over to the It Clique corner in the courtyard.

Skye's emerald-coloured eyes narrowed mischievously at me, almost as if she was looking for a place of vulnerability. I could tell she wanted to screw with me that day, but I wasn't going to let her have it,

MY MIAMI 1992 - JANUARY (NEW YEAR, NEW DRAMA)

instead, I was going to stay calm and collected.

Meghan hadn't arrived yet, so I knew Skye was going to be up to no good.

"Meghan and I had *soooo* much fun yesterday!" Skye said in an over-exaggerated tone, "Aww! Too bad you weren't there."

"Huh?" I asked, pretending to be uninterested, "Sorry, I wasn't listening."

"She said she was going to invite you - but you weren't available," she said in a sweet cheery voice.

"Skye, I know you're lying," I scoffed, "You weren't even supposed to go out yesterday, it was like 91 degrees."

"Believe whatever you want," Skye shrugged.

"I'll ask Meghan, when she comes, if she says no, I'll tell her you're a liar," I warned.

"I'm not a liar, but fine," Skye had no sign of fear on her face.

Was she really telling the truth?

*****

I saw Talia that morning during history class, but she was nowhere to be found during lunch period. That was odd. All middle schoolers were expected to have lunch in the cafeteria.

MY MIAMI 1992 - JANUARY (NEW YEAR, NEW DRAMA)

As I was getting my lunch, I accidentally bumped into Charlotte. She wobbled and almost spilled her lunch tray on the floor but saved it just in time.

"Watch where you're going!" she snapped.

Great. Now I had two It Clique members against me, Skye and Charlotte.

I quickly apologized, and with extra caution, I walked slowly to the It Clique table with my lunch tray firmly in my hands.

"Woah! That was close," Meghan laughed (she had seen the collision between Charlotte and I). "It's burning in here, I'm about to melt."

"Same!" Rosalyn and Emerald exhaled at the same time.

I smiled. As much as I enjoyed the chill vibe at the It Clique table, I needed to confront Meghan about what Skye had told me.

"Did Skye come over to your house yesterday?" I asked, interrupting Emerald, Rosalyn, and Meghan's small talk.

"Umm..." Meghan said fiddling with her straw, "I-"

Meghan was interrupted by Skye who placed her tray loudly on the table.

MY MIAMI 1992 - JANUARY (NEW YEAR, NEW DRAMA)

"It was so much fun hanging out yesterday, we should do it more often!" Skye said to Meghan, then she glared at me. "Too bad Jennifer wasn't available."

"What do you mean? Nobody even called me," I said, looking at Meghan suspiciously.

"We talked on the phone yesterday, Jen," Meghan pointed out.

"Okay, but you never said anything about coming over," I scoffed.

"Yes, I did," she lied.

"Why are you lying?!" I yelled.

"Stop it Jennifer, you're making a scene," Charlotte scolded me.

Students at the other tables began to stare at us, but I didn't care. Meghan had lied to me several times that week, and I was getting sick and tired of it.

"I didn't even do anything to you. I just didn't invite you over," Meghan protested, raising her voice. "It's not even that big of a deal."

"Well, you lied to me *and* Skye," I said back, even louder than before, "Now you're just making yourself look bad."

"Hey, don't involve me in this," Skye interjected nervously.

MY MIAMI 1992 - JANUARY (NEW YEAR, NEW DRAMA)

"Skye wasn't even supposed to tell you that," Meghan yelled, focusing her eyes on Skye.

"Oh, so now you're keeping secrets with Skye. I thought I was your best friend!" I whined. I knew that I sounded like a baby, but I didn't care.

"You know what, Jennifer? Just forget it. I don't want to talk about this anymore," Meghan waved her hand dismissively at me.

Meghan then stood up and walked over to another table. Everyone else packed up their stuff and followed her without a word. What was it that made everyone so terrified of her? Why was I terrified of her? What did Meghan have that everyone regarded her like she was the boss of the school?

How could they be on her side? She was the one who had lied. Right to my face! I had no allies here. What was I even doing here with these girls?

MY MIAMI 1992 - JANUARY (NEW YEAR, NEW DRAMA)

Friday, January 10th, 1992

I came back home that day feeling discouraged. I needed to begin my research on Rayne Weaver and the little information I had wasn't helping. Seeing the way Meghan was beginning to act "funny"; I didn't want to put all my eggs in the "Meghan basket".

I needed a plan B, and what better plan than Rayne Weaver's daughter, Talia. But, where in the world did she go? I hadn't seen her anywhere at school that day.

As I was writing my plan for my Rayne Weaver biography, I received a call from the one and only Meghan Benjaminson. Fantastic!

I was surprised that she called, because Meghan had basically ghosted me the entire day during lunch.

"Talia and her dad came over to my house today," she said without saying hello, "I thought you might want to know."

Oh, my goodness. I needed to get to Meghan's house that instant. This was my chance!

"I'm coming over right now! Just let me ask my mom -," I started.

"Jennifer! Did you not hear me?" Meghan interrupted, "I said she *came* to my house, she left like an hour ago."

MY MIAMI 1992 - JANUARY (NEW YEAR, NEW DRAMA)

I took a deep breath, "And you're just telling me this now? Meghan, what the heck!"

"Oh, don't be so fresh," she snapped, "I just forgot to tell you while she was here; she was only at my house for like 20 minutes."

"Fine. What was she there for?"

"Well, I don't know exactly, but apparently he was giving my dad some information about your little author," Meghan informed me, "It sounded like a kind of serious discussion."

"What do you mean?"

"Like I'm not one to eavesdrop, but from what I heard they were talking about legal stuff," Meghan said slowly.

I smiled. For the first time in the past couple of days Meghan was being a good friend and providing me with the information that I needed.

We chatted about other things for a little bit and before Meghan was able to hang up, I said, "Hey Meghan?"

"Yeah?"

"Thanks."

"For what?"

MY MIAMI 1992 - JANUARY (NEW YEAR, NEW DRAMA)

"For telling me this, I'm glad you came to me first," I thanked her. Did this mean Meghan and I were on good terms now?

Meghan didn't say anything, but to continue the conversation and get her to speak, I decided to apologize about the other day.

"Also, I'm sorry for shouting at you in the cafeteria, I just felt kind of left out by you and Skye," I told her, "But I know that I shouldn't have felt that way since I'm your best friend. I'm so sorry that I over-reacted."

"Okay," Meghan said blankly, "Thanks for the apology."

"Besties?" I asked with a laugh.

"Sure."

Meghan's response did not convince me. She didn't return my energy the way she normally did whenever we agreed on something. Her tone was making me think that she was still unhappy with me.

Before I could say anything, Meghan quickly told me that she had to go; but before she hung up, I heard something that I could recognize from miles away. Rosalyn's laugh. She had a very high pitched and unique laugh that really stuck to her.

Meghan wasn't even that close to Rosalyn, so it couldn't be just the two of them hanging out. Meghan was most likely hanging out with the entire It Clique. Why didn't

MY MIAMI 1992 - JANUARY (NEW YEAR, NEW DRAMA)

she invite me? I was also a member of the It Clique… Right?

MY MIAMI 1992 - JANUARY (NEW YEAR, NEW DRAMA)

Saturday, January 11th, 1992

That afternoon, I went for a bike ride around the neighborhood to de-stress from all the petty It Clique drama. So many things were running through my mind about what was going on, I began to even wonder why I was in the It Clique in the first place.

The way Meghan was behaving was so bizarre, one day we were fine, and the next she acted as if she didn't even want me around. If Meghan didn't want me in the It Clique - I had no place being there at all.

I stopped by a playground and sat myself on the grass. I watched a few kids play a game of grounders. Every now and then new kids would arrive, introduce themselves, and ask if they could play. One of the girls who seemed to be "in charge" of it all, welcomed each child in with grace.

As I was watching, I thought of the It Clique once again. How if I'd want to make a new group of friends (like the kids who wanted to join the game of grounders), I'd first go to Meghan to see if she liked them. Loyalty was incredibly crucial to Meghan. A flare of bitterness entered me.

Meghan sat on a pedestal bossing us around and telling us who we could and couldn't be friends with so much, that I didn't really have any other friends at school. Before I started hanging out with the It Clique, I had multiple, but now all I had was Meghan and people who would do anything not to have me around. I had so many valuable

MY MIAMI 1992 - JANUARY (NEW YEAR, NEW DRAMA)

friendships, but the minute Meghan told me who she did and didn't like I obliged and immediately stopped talking to them.

I felt awful. The feeling of guilt grew even more when I thought of my one particular friend - Carolyn Howard.

I stared at the playground… I had no friends.

That had to change - sooner or later.

It made sense for the It Clique to probably get to the point of kicking me out. Quite frankly, the only reason I was in the It Clique was because of my friendship with Meghan. With that friendship hanging by a thread, it made no sense for me to remain in the It Clique. My status as "Meghan's best friend" was on its way down the drains.

I suddenly sensed an urgent need to begin to mend all my old broken friendships. I needed to make more friends and not be so clingy to Meghan all the time. Maybe if I started hanging out with other people Meghan would realize what a great friend, I was to her.

MY MIAMI 1992 - JANUARY (NEW YEAR, NEW DRAMA)

Sunday, January 12th, 1992

Dear Rayne Weaver,

Hello again. I haven't sent you a letter for a couple of days now because I've been in some friendship drama. I know you probably won't see this, but I wanted to ask you regardless. What do you do if you have a friend who keeps lying to you, and you don't know if you can trust? What would you do? If you reply to it would mean the world to me.

Jennifer Chevrolet

After we got back from church that Sunday, my family and I were invited to a picnic by a few of our church family friends at the famous South Beach in Miami. Living in the Grove, my family and I probably went to South Beach at least once a month and always a fun experience.

It was a nice picnic with lots of food including burgers, hotdogs, salad, etc. For the most part, I hung out by the water with the younger kids (no one my age was there) until I got bored and decided I needed another hotdog and returned to where the parents were sitting.

As I ate my hotdog, I sat at a distance away from the parents, but close enough that I could easily hear their conversations. I didn't plan to eavesdrop, but I couldn't stop myself from hearing them.

"Sooo... Adeline, what's it like living in a condominium?" Mrs. Collymore asked my mom. "I would feel so claustrophobic in a

MY MIAMI 1992 - JANUARY (NEW YEAR, NEW DRAMA)

small place like that, it's so full of different kinds of people. I hope you have a ton of security cameras."

I watched as my mother laughed it off as if it were nothing. That was *so* rude. I couldn't believe that Mrs. Collymore was mocking my mom for living in a condo. We weren't less than her because we didn't experience the rich-kid suburban life she did!

I'd never heard someone speak to my mom in that manner; did she get these kinds of questions every day? Just because we didn't live in the suburbs like she did. I was enraged.

"Well, it's just been tight lately with the kids' school," my mom told her.

"Wow, that must be a huge financial pain, right?" she remarked. "How can you even afford such a top-notch school? Coconut Grove Academy? I know it's none of my business, but we are talking like 15 grand per year. Right? You need a nicer house Adeline, maybe you should try a public school instead?" Mrs. Collymore went on and on.

Under my breath, I muttered, "You're right; it is none of your business", but not loud enough for the adults to hear.

I was very astonished the by the way Mrs. Collymore was talking to my mom, she always seemed so kind and down to earth. But I guess people are not always what they seem.

MY MIAMI 1992 - JANUARY (NEW YEAR, NEW DRAMA)

"We focus our financial attention on our kids' education, Cassie. Our kids are fine just the way they are. They're growing up quite nicely. Education is the most important to us right now," my dad chipped in.

He seemed visibly annoyed that Mrs. Collymore was barging into our personal business for no good reason.

"We should start a charity in church for you guys in that case. I mean I drove by your address with my little one, and I don't know if I can have Jennifer being friends with my little Kylie if your home is in that state-" Mrs. Collymore started.

"Charity? Really Cassie? What in the world has gotten into you?" my mom chided her.

"Look, we don't need charity, we are doing absolutely fine, okay?" my dad said with a crisp tone. Things were getting heated and I could feel the tension in my bones.

Mrs. Collymore laughed, "No, I was just kidding!"

My dad gave her a long hard look but said nothing. My mom did the same. Then the adults went back to what appeared to be a normal boring conversation.

"How rude!" I muttered under my breath.

The situation made me so mad, but more determined than ever to win the Project Authors challenge. It was due next month and the clock was ticking. I couldn't let

MY MIAMI 1992 - JANUARY (NEW YEAR, NEW DRAMA)

anyone stop me now, not even Meghan Benjaminson and all her drama. It was time for me to get fired up and on a roll. Life is a chess game and to win you've got to make a move. And Jennifer Alexis Chevrolet is going to make that move.

MY MIAMI 1992 - JANUARY (NEW YEAR, NEW DRAMA)

Monday, January 13th, 1992

I woke up extra early that morning so I could meet up with one of the It Clique members other than Skye and Meghan. I made sure my dad rushed through the Miami traffic just to get me to school fifteen minutes before the bell.

I arrived at school to see Emerald sitting by herself on the self-proclaimed It Clique benches. She was fiddling with her pink Walkman and quietly observing everyone in the courtyard.

I liked Emerald. We weren't close at all, but I liked her spirit. She wasn't too proud or vain like Skye, not too secretive like Charlotte, not too talkative like Rosalyn, or too fake like Meghan. She spoke when she was spoken to and was very selective in what she chose to say. When Emerald spoke, we all listened.

I was glad that I was going to be alone with her, because I wanted to ask about the It Clique hanging out on Friday.

"Hey Emerald!" I called, walking up to her.

She looked up at me and waved. We had some quick small talk, then I went straight to the chase, "Did you and the rest of the group go to Meghan's house on Friday?"

I kept my fingers crossed behind my back that Emerald would be honest with me. Hopefully Meghan or Skye hadn't convinced her to keep it a secret from me.

MY MIAMI 1992 - JANUARY (NEW YEAR, NEW DRAMA)

"Yeah, why?"

I took a deep breath of relief. Finally, someone was being honest!

"I wasn't invited and I'm not really sure why," I told her.

"What do you mean you're not sure why?!" Emerald said, suddenly sharpening her tone. "Didn't you and Meghan get in a fight?"

"Yeah - But we made up - over the phone," I stammered.

Emerald was about to say something when Skye walked over and looked me up and down, "Wow – you've got lots of nerve to be sitting with us."

"Oh my gosh, Skye, chill out - Meghan and I made up already," I snapped while rolling my eyes.

"I know."

"So then what's your problem?" I asked.

"Meghan said she doesn't know if she wants to be friends with you anymore, since you like *really* embarrassed her on Friday," Skye told me.

I knew that I couldn't trust a word Skye said - ever.

"Look Skye, we made up. Meghan's not even mad anymore, I'm super sure. I know Meghan way better than you do."

MY MIAMI 1992 - JANUARY (NEW YEAR, NEW DRAMA)

"You're so desperate to be Meghan's BFF! If you didn't have us, you'd have no friends."

"Whatever," I said, pretending not to care.

Skye was right. I would have no friends if it wasn't for the It Clique. However, I wasn't going to admit it and give the benefit of being right.

At this point, with my new focus on winning the Author's Project challenge, I needed to avoid all the distractions from the It Clique. I hadn't paid much attention to my research that weekend, therefore every minute was becoming precious. There was no time to waste. I needed to somehow figure out how to leave the It Clique, but I didn't have the guts to do it yet.

Skye didn't say anything and sat down beside Emerald. I was watching Mrs. B's car park in the distance when Talia ran over to me and grabbed my arm, "I need to talk to you."

I was taken by surprise. What was going on with Talia? She hadn't been at school for the past few days, and suddenly, it seemed as if something was wrong.

"What? Are you okay?" I let her pull me over to the field. At the corner of my eye, I watched Meghan walk over to the group.

"Where are you going?" she mouthed when she saw me with Talia. I raised my shoulders. Meghan gave me a questionable look and returned her attention to the It Clique.

MY MIAMI 1992 - JANUARY (NEW YEAR, NEW DRAMA)

When we got to a secluded corner Talia looked at me and said, "Stop sending letters to my mom."

"Huh?"

"Look. What I am about to tell you, you can't tell anyone. Anyone."

"Okay, okay, go on," I answered impatiently. What was happening?

"It's been me responding to your letters with my mom's traditional fan mail letters. I didn't know how she would respond to those letters, so I've just been sending people those ones. It's also been me delivering them to your house."

I was taken aback. Rayne Weaver had no idea I was writing her letters. All of that time I spent composing letters was for nothing.

"Wait- I'm so confused, why would you need to do that for your mom?"

"It's kind of complicated, but my parents separated and are getting a divorce. My Mom lives in Louisiana. Before my parents separated, they had already bought the house that we live in right now and set everything up for us to move. My mom made that our permanent address so that all her fan mail could go there. Then things started going sideways and my parents decided to get a divorce. So, when we moved, we kept on receiving mail from her fans, so I decided to read a few and respond to them. I then noticed how you've been sending a lot to her, so I thought I

MY MIAMI 1992 - JANUARY (NEW YEAR, NEW DRAMA)

might just tell you, that there is probably zero chance that my mom will come across your letter."

I was taken aback with unfathomable horror. I felt like I'd been smacked by a ton of bricks! My entire investigation - all of my efforts - was completely futile. I had practically wasted the past two weeks of the new year sending letters like crazy to someone who wasn't even receiving or reading them. I wasted my time.

I thanked Talia for giving me the bombshell, and slowly walked back to the It Clique, in a daze.

"Oh my gosh! Jennifer, you look like you saw a ghost or something," Rosalyn said, as I approached them.

"Well?" Meghan said putting her hands on her hips, "What did Talia say?"

Talia had warned me not to tell anybody, and I didn't want to betray her confidence, especially since we've only known each other for a short time. I was going to keep it a secret as I had promised and not tell Meghan. Besides, Meghan was always keeping secrets from and making me feel excluded. She wasn't a good friend, and I didn't trust her anymore.

"Um... She said I can't tell you," I said, staring past Meghan into the distant horizon, "And I really don't feel like talking right now, if you don't mind."

MY MIAMI 1992 - JANUARY (NEW YEAR, NEW DRAMA)

Meghan went silent for a minute then said, "Oh - that's alright, come on let's go to a corner, then you can tell me."

"I can't tell you, Meghan. I can't tell anyone," I stood my ground.

"Why not?" Meghan demanded. She crossed her arms and glared at me, while the rest of the It Clique did the same.

"Cause - I don't want to. It's a secret, okay?" I stammered.

"What a great excuse, Jennifer," Meghan exclaimed sarcastically while throwing her hands in the air.

"I'm sorry, I really am, okay? I promised Talia to keep it a secret. It doesn't even make sense why you are so upset. You keep secrets from me all the time!" I said.

"Jennifer, just get out of my sight, and don't sit with us at lunch today."

Meghan was angry with me. That was clear. What wasn't clear was if she was kicking me out of the It Clique. In my innermost mind, I wanted out anyway. I was tired of all the unnecessary drama.

All I cared about was how to deal with and process what Talia just told me. How in the world can I get to Rayne Weaver now?

*****

At lunch, I was planning to sit beside Talia so we could talk more about her mom.

MY MIAMI 1992 - JANUARY (NEW YEAR, NEW DRAMA)

I searched all over the cafeteria for her until I saw her sitting at the It Clique table ... beside Meghan ... My spot. What was she doing over there?

Was Talia trying to take my place in the It Clique? Or was Meghan using her to make me jealous? Talia seemed to be truly trying to help me, so I inclined toward the second scenario. She probably didn't realize what she was getting herself into with Meghan. I kept my fingers crossed as I sat alone at a table, praying that Talia wouldn't let the It Clique corrupt her.

MY MIAMI 1992 - JANUARY (NEW YEAR, NEW DRAMA)

Tuesday, January 14th, 1992

At lunch I was busy working on an important English project, so I only saw Meghan once that day during school in the hallway. We didn't say anything; just stared past each other and went about our business.

When I was home from school and finishing up some homework, I was surprised to receive a phone call from her.

"Hi Meghan."

"You can tell me now Jennifer, I'm all alone in my room and I promise I won't tell anyone," she said.

"Meghan - It's not that easy," I said nervously, "Talia is my friend, and I wouldn't want to betray her trust like that."

"Your friend? Seriously Jen? You only met her like last week; she has a terrible attitude, and you're calling her your friend? You just want to be friends with her to get connected with her mom!" Meghan yelled. "It doesn't make any sense! Why is this random author so important to you?!"

"First off, how about you stop yelling," I said with a dangerous tone in my voice (practically imitating my mom when she angry), "And second, it's none of your business."

"Well, it is going to be my business if you ever want to come to my house to find out

MY MIAMI 1992 - JANUARY (NEW YEAR, NEW DRAMA)

more about Rayne Weaver from my dad," Meghan warned mischievously.

"You're being so petty right now Meghan!" I exclaimed.

"I'm being petty. I'm being petty?" Meghan repeated to herself loudly. "You're the one keeping secrets!"

"Well, now you know what it feels like."

"Excuse me?"

"You keep secrets from me all the time! You also host hangouts with the It Clique without me, and you talk about me behind my back. So, tell me, how does the taste of your own medicine feel?"

"So that's how it is?" Meghan asked with a calm voice.

"Yeah."

"Alright then. Goodbye Jennifer Chevrolet," Meghan scoffed.

"Goodbye Meghan Benjaminson," I replied returning the same energy.

I quickly hung up on Meghan before she could say anything else or hang up on me instead.

I wanted to be angry. I wanted to be outraged at Meghan for being such a hypocrite. I even wanted to be happy that I had left the most toxic group to ever exist. But instead, I was sad, because I

MY MIAMI 1992 - JANUARY (NEW YEAR, NEW DRAMA)

knew I had lost a friendship that would take forever to get back, if at all.

I was alone.

My thoughts were interrupted by my mom calling my brother and I downstairs for supper. Not really being in the mood to eat, I sluggishly walked downstairs. Once I got my plate I began to fiddle around with my fork and barely touched my food. I had lost my appetite.

"Hey! What's wrong with you, sweetie?" my mom asked as she sat beside me at the dining table.

"Nothing," I shrugged.

I looked at Martin who shook his head disapprovingly at me. Rude.

"She got into a fight with Meghan," Martin told her. "I heard her."

I stared at Martin angrily. He had been eavesdropping on my conversation. I understood that with our small house it wasn't that hard to hear someone's conversation in the next room, but Martin had no right or reason to say anything. I kicked him underneath the table.

"Ouch!" he groaned.

"What happened?" Mom asked curiously.

I suddenly became irritated. Why was my mom suddenly so interested in anything related to me? What happened to talking about

MY MIAMI 1992 - JANUARY (NEW YEAR, NEW DRAMA)

Martin's sports team or his grades? That was all we ever spoke about at dinner. What was with the newfound interest?

"It's fine. I don't want to talk about it," I said.

"Woah! Attitude. I see someone's becoming a teenager!" my dad laughed.

I cringed, as my family cackled. The joke wasn't even funny.

I rolled my eyes, quickly gobbled up my meal and went straight back up to my room.

I was so upset. I turned on my radio and blasted upbeat funk music. At times, music was the only thing that could calm me down. It was always there for me and helped uplift my mood whenever I needed it.

I knew that I was going to get in trouble for blasting music in the house, but I didn't care. At that moment, I needed the music to be louder thoughts.

My mom burst into my room, "Jennifer!"

I paused my music. "Can you knock?" I said with an annoyed tone in my voice.

"You better watch that tone, young lady."

What was my mom's problem? Couldn't she just leave me alone?

"What's going on with you today?" she demanded.

MY MIAMI 1992 - JANUARY (NEW YEAR, NEW DRAMA)

I groaned. There was no point in hiding. I wasn't going to be left alone until I told her.

I explained to her how Meghan was turning into a pathological liar, that I didn't feel like I belonged in the It Clique, how I was kicked out, and how I stood up to Meghan the other day. Obviously, there was more to the story, but I didn't want to tell her. I left Rayne Weaver and Talia completely out of it.

"Oh honey! I had no idea you were going through all that," my mom sympathized, "I'm so glad you finally stood up for yourself."

"How could you?" I thought. She and dad were always concerned about Martin and his problems. I was constantly overlooked because I was the youngest.

"I know, but now I just feel bad for myself, since I have no friends at school now."

I felt my eyes begin to water. *Don't cry, don't cry, don't cry.*

"I'm so proud of you for standing up for yourself honey," she repeated, "It's important to be assertive, and know when you are being played."

"Yeah, but I don't want to be friendless. Maybe I should just apologize," I muttered, biting my nails.

Talking with my mom was making me way more upset than I wanted to be. I was definitely

MY MIAMI 1992 - JANUARY (NEW YEAR, NEW DRAMA)

mad at Meghan, but there were still droplets of blue beneath all of the red.

"Don't let being lonely make you reconnect with toxic people, Jennifer. You shouldn't drink poison, just because you are thirsty," my mom warned.

My mother's words struck me like a bolt of lightning. Suddenly, thoughts I had back at the park started recycling in my mind all over again.

I was done with the It Clique, and I was done with Meghan Benjaminson. I wasn't going to let her control me anymore.

And *that* was how I found my second new year's resolution. Who said you couldn't have two?

MY MIAMI 1992 - JANUARY (NEW YEAR, NEW DRAMA)

Wednesday, January 15th, 1992

I was nervous about going to school that day, but I was also happy since a tiny lioness was growing inside of me. I felt courageous, and even though I was a little terrified, my bravery triumphed.

As I stepped into the school courtyard, I noticed the It Clique staring at me intently. Crossed arms, up and down stares, and their leader in front, with hands on her hips, intensely glaring at me. Classic.

As I stared back at them, I felt a pang of guilt. The week before, that would have been me. Following Meghan's orders like a robot and accompanying her while she worked hard to make someone's school life unpleasant. I was relieved that I wouldn't be a part of that any longer. They were all just a gang of bullies, and I didn't want that for myself.

An example of an It Clique victim was Carolyn Howard, an old friend of mine. Carolyn and I were inseparable, until Meghan and I became friends in the fourth grade. Meghan didn't like Carolyn and that I couldn't hang out with her anymore if I wanted to be part of the It Clique. Foolishly, I agreed and pretended as though Carolyn didn't exist. Looking back at that moment made me feel terrible.

I couldn't believe how many friendships I'd lost because of Meghan. I thought that she was looking out for me, but instead she was just manipulating me to do whatever she wanted. Meghan was never a true friend to

MY MIAMI 1992 - JANUARY (NEW YEAR, NEW DRAMA)

me and in some way, it made me think higher of Skye. At least Skye made it known that she didn't value me and saw me as a puppet. It was better to have an honest foe than a fake friend.

I took a glance at Skye. She was smiling. It must have been the greatest moment of her life. She had succeeded. Meghan and I were no longer friends, making her Meghan's official new bestie. However, I didn't care anymore about Skye, Meghan, or anyone else in that group. They weren't my problem anymore.

*****

When I arrived at the cafeteria, I ran into Talia filling up her lunch tray.

"Hey Talia! Wanna sit with me?" I asked cheerfully. According to my knowledge, Talia wasn't an official member of the It Clique, so she was free to mingle with whoever she wanted.

She looked as if she was going to say yes until someone interrupted her.

"Talia!" called a familiar voice.

I spun around to see Meghan waving from the It Clique table.

"Come sit with us!" she said grinning at me mischievously.

Ugh. I knew that Meghan only wanted to be best friends with Talia to get back at me.

MY MIAMI 1992 - JANUARY (NEW YEAR, NEW DRAMA)

But I knew it could never happen. Talia was astute and couldn't be duped by anyone.

Talia looked at me and shrugged, "Welp, there's always tomorrow, Chevrolet. See ya later alligator!"

I stood there in shock as Talia patted my shoulder and walked over to the It Clique table. Why was she adhering to Meghan's cruel bindings?

Meghan graciously directed Talia to Skye's spot (which was across from her) Skye marched herself to my seat with pride. It was official. Jennifer Chevrolet's spot in the It Clique was officially replaced.

I strolled over to an empty table. As I ate my lunch, I watched Talia and the It Clique laugh and chat as if they were one big happy family.

That stung.

MY MIAMI 1992 - JANUARY (NEW YEAR, NEW DRAMA)

Thursday, January 16th, 1992

It was one of the best and worst days of my life. Best because I seemed to have reconnected with an old friend and worst because Meghan embarrassed me in front of the whole grade.

Actually, before reconnecting with an old friend, I had another good moment in the day during recess...

I was quietly in the corner of the courtyard reading a Rayne Weaver book, while all my hopes in the Project Author's challenge were slowly fading away. Once I got to the climax, Talia came up and sat beside me.

I shut my book and looked at her deep in the eyes, "So you're done hanging out with the mean girls now?"

"Chill out Chevrolet," she laughed dismissively, "I wanted to tell you about this party I'm having next Saturday, it's going to be super fun."

I grunted, "Let me guess, the It Clique is going to be there?"

"Yeah, but I'm inviting you because my mom is going to be there."

I put my book to the side. I wasn't sure whether I should believe Talia. She hung out with two of the biggest liars in the school. How was I supposed to know if she could be trusted?

MY MIAMI 1992 - JANUARY (NEW YEAR, NEW DRAMA)

"Look, I know you probably don't believe me, but just think about it, okay?" Talia said, "By the way there's no guarantee that she's going to be there."

"Thought so," I grunted. "What's the occasion of the party?"

"It's just my birthday, I'm turning 13, you know how everyone is about having a 13th birthday party," Talia told me excitedly, "My mom is just going to pop in to wish me happy birthday and cut the cake."

"Sweet!" I said gently, pretending not to be too excited, even though I was.

Talia handed me an invitation card and ordered me not to inform the It Clique that I had been invited, even though I had no intention of doing so.

When Talia walked away, I smiled to myself. It was so kind of her to invite me! This would be my opportunity to meet Rayne Weaver face to face!

Talia Weaver's 13th Birthday Party!

Date: Saturday, January 25th, 1992

Time: 6:00PM – 9:00PM

Place: 132 Boulevard Street, Miami, Florida (Talia's House)

RSVP: Talia Weaver (202-555-0313)

MY MIAMI 1992 - JANUARY (NEW YEAR, NEW DRAMA)

*****

All of the drama at Coconut Grove Academy began in the cafeteria. It was practically a tradition.

My obstinate math instructor would not allow me to leave the classroom for lunch until I had correctly answered all the questions on my assignment, so I arrived a little later than usual. Meghan appeared to be late as well, so as I was filling up my tray, Meghan was behind me, with just one person between us.

When I saw how close Meghan was to me, I hurried to fetch my meal, almost splashing guacamole all over my shoes.

I realized that I had forgotten to grab some corn chips, and turned to grab some, just to get face to face with Meghan. Where had the guy in between us gone?

"Sorry," I stammered trying to get behind her.

"Move it Chevrolet," she pounced.

I hurriedly collected my chips and dashed to the table where I had sat the day before. I was on my way to the table when I thought I heard Talia's voice behind me. I turned around only to see Meghan walking in my direction with her tray, not looking where she was going.

Bong! She and her guacamole smacked into me. I was a jumbled mess. It had gotten everywhere!

MY MIAMI 1992 - JANUARY (NEW YEAR, NEW DRAMA)

What was Meghan up to? The It Clique's table was nowhere near mine. Why was she even walking in my general direction?

"Meghan!" I yelled, "What are you doing?"

"Whoops! Sorry!" Meghan giggled mischievously.

"What is your problem!" I yelled again, "Just leave me alone, I did nothing to you!"

"Oh don't be such a baby," she laughed.

The It Clique peered over from their table to glance at what was happening. They all began to laugh hysterically (except for Talia) but stopped when the lunch lady came over to help me.

The lunch lady yelled at Meghan, who merely pretended it was a mistake. What an evil little rascal! There was no way she didn't do that on purpose.

I walked out of the cafeteria, fully convinced that everyone's eyes were glued on me. Meghan was pushing my buttons harder and harder by the day. She wasn't going to stop until she saw me crumble and beg for mercy. If this was the way she wanted to play, I was going to play along.

I entered the girls' restroom, trying to wash out all the guacamole from my hair by using a wet paper towel, when Carolyn Howard (my old friend) walked in.

MY MIAMI 1992 - JANUARY (NEW YEAR, NEW DRAMA)

"Jennifer! Your hair! I saw what happened. That Meghan girl is an absolute jerk," she said, "Do you need help?"

"That would be great, thank you," I said, passing her a paper towel.

Carolyn helped clean my hair in silence.

"It's been quite a while since we've hung out," Carolyn said, breaking the silence.

"I know and I want to just say I'm sorry about -," I began to say.

"It's okay, I understand…," Carolyn interrupted. "Do you maybe want to come over to my place tomorrow? I'm pretty sure our moms still have each other's numbers."

"Sure!" I said without even thinking.

I was a little shocked by Carolyn's forgiveness and invitation, but I was so glad that we had reconciled. It overshadowed the embarrassment that Meghan had put me through.

Carolyn and I spent the rest of the lunch break catching up on everything we missed after not talking for three years. It felt so good to have her back.

I left school that day beaming at the fact that I had made a new friend. I wasn't so alone after all!

MY MIAMI 1992 - JANUARY (NEW YEAR, NEW DRAMA)

Friday, January 17th, 1992

I spent that day at school hanging out with Carolyn and her friends Lyla and Florence. I knew Lyla from my science class, but I had never really met Florence, besides seeing her a few times in the hallway. The girls were courteous and welcomed me in open arms. It felt so refreshing, but also kind of weird to be in a non-toxic environment. This was a change.

To my surprise, Meghan took a break from bothering me that day and only gave the stink I when she saw me in the cafeteria. However, I didn't care, I had three new friends that made me feel like I meant something. Something that Meghan or anyone in the It Clique could never do for me. I was better without them.

*****

My Mom dropped me off at Carolyn's house that afternoon to spend the evening with her and her family. I hadn't been to Carolyn's house for so long, taking the ten-minute drive to her averagely sized house brought back so many memories.

I rang the doorbell of her house with my mom behind me and Ms. Howard opened the door.

"Hi Jennifer! Long time no see!" Ms. Howard gave me a huge hug. "Adeline! How have you been?"

MY MIAMI 1992 - JANUARY (NEW YEAR, NEW DRAMA)

My mom and I entered the Howard residence. I was surprised to find Carolyn watching TV with a boy I didn't recognize. Carolyn only had one sister, Lanaya.

Carolyn stood up from the couch, gave me a hug, and introduced me to the mystery boy - Arthur.

"My mom got engaged this Christmas," Carolyn explained to me as we sat down on the couch. "Arthur, William, and Nick are my future stepbrother's. They go to a different school than us, Arthur's seven, William's ten, and Nicholas is thirteen."

"That's amazing!" I exclaimed, I then lowered my voice so Arthur who was right beside us wouldn't hear me, "How do you feel about that?"

Carolyn was a beautiful chocolate brown-skinned girl with chestnut-coloured eyes and thick curly hair in braids. She lost her dad when she was just seven years old and living in Wisconsin. Carolyn seldom talked about it, but whenever it came up, it always made her unhappy. So, it was natural for Carolyn to feel strange with her new family. For so long, it had been just her, her mom, and younger sister Lanaya. But I always knew Carolyn to be one of the strongest people that I knew. She could take on anything.

"At first, I didn't like my stepdad, David Milton, but as I got to know him more, he wasn't as horrible as I made him out to be," Carolyn said as she stared down at her socks. She then looked up at me and smiled, "I'm just glad he makes my mom happy."

"Carolyn Milton kind of has a ring to it," I teased to lighten up the mood.

"Very funny. My mom says I don't have to change my last name," Carolyn said before playfully whacked me.

"Are they going to have a wedding?"

"Yep, in March, Lanaya and I are going to be flower girls, since we're too young to be bridesmaids," Carolyn informed me, "We're going to be moving into their house, until we find a home big enough for all seven of us. So, I have to share a room with my sister for a few months."

Carolyn blanched at the prospect of sharing a room with Lanaya, and I chuckled. I looked around me, my mom and Ms. Howard were conversing in the kitchen, Arthur's eyes were riveted to the TV, while Carolyn was making me laugh with her embarrassing stories about her stepbrothers (two of whom weren't even there).

I felt like I belonged for the first time in a while.

Saturday, January 18th, 1992

"Hello?" Talia said when she picked up the phone.

I needed to give Talia a crucial phone call that Saturday morning. I had to ask if it was okay for me to bring Carolyn to her birthday party, so I could rub it in Skye and Meghan's face that I didn't need friends like them anymore.

"Hey Talia! It's me, Jennifer. I'm calling to let you know that I'll be at your party next week."

"Cool! I told my mom about the letters you've been sending her; she said when she comes to Miami, she'll pick up her letters... and redirect all future mail to her address in Louisiana. So, there's some good news for you."

"Omg! Thank you, Talia! You're the best!"

"I know."

I laughed. Talia had quite an interesting character. Her actions proved that she was a kind and compassionate individual, yet at times her words suggested otherwise.

"Anyway, I was also calling to ask if I could bring a friend with me."

"Who?"

"Carolyn Howard."

MY MIAMI 1992 - JANUARY (NEW YEAR, NEW DRAMA)

"Carolyn?" Talia pondered, "Ah well, I guess it wouldn't kill anyone to have *one* extra guest."

"Thanks Talia!"

"You owe me."

"I know," I laughed.

"I mean it. Goodbye Chevrolet."

I gulped. I wasn't exactly sure what she meant by me owing her. It wasn't as if I had begged her to be invited. What exactly did I owe?

I decided not to dwell on what Talia had said and shifted my attention towards a trick I had up my sleeve. Throughout the day, I came up with an amazing idea to show Meghan who was "boss" around here…

A massive 13th birthday party... *pour moi!*

MY MIAMI 1992 - JANUARY (NEW YEAR, NEW DRAMA)

Sunday, January 19th, 1992

That Sunday at church, Martin, Meghan, and I attended our regular youth group sessions and discussed how Judas betrayed Jesus for 30 pieces of silver.

Mrs. Edwood (our team leader) asked, "Describe a time where you felt betrayed by someone you trusted. How did it feel?"

Great. It was time for our circle discussions and Meghan was up first. She squinted her eyes at me.

"I was betrayed by someone I used to call my best friend. It hurt. *A lot*. We promised each other never to keep secrets. And she betrayed that promise. I'm not sure how or if I'll be able to forgive her."

I gulped. Meghan said every word staring directly at me. You could cut the tension in the room with a knife.

A few people went ahead with their stories, then it was finally my turn. Time to fight fire with fire.

"Similar to Meghan's story, I was also betrayed by my former best friend. She was a horrible friend to me and had a hugely inflated ego. She also purposely tried to isolate me from others, simply because she didn't find any interest in anyone but herself," I said looking at Meghan the same way she had looked at me. I then turned my attention to Mrs. Edwood, "But I'm so glad I was able to get myself out of such a destructive friendship and learn that not everyone wants the best for you."

I looked at Meghan who sat there looking at her feet in silence. She did not say another word for the rest of the session.

I grinned with contentment. Take that Benjaminson!

MY MIAMI 1992 - JANUARY (NEW YEAR, NEW DRAMA)

Monday, January 20th, 1992

It was Martin Luther King Jr. Day, a public holiday, meaning that most business, including schools, were closed. It also meant that I would be able to spend a full day without having to see Meghan Benjaminson's face.

I had intended on spending being lazy but was forced out of it when my mom demanded that I cleaned her room. Once I finished, I began to write down a message to my parents, pleading for my dream 13th birthday party.

Dear Mom and Dad,

I want you to know that you are the very BEST parents ever! I love you for everything! So, I'm going to be thirteen soon... And I was thinking maybe I could have a birthday party! I'm open to using some of my allowance money to pay for it, but I would really, really appreciate it, if you let me throw this party. I really hope you say yes.

Your daughter Jen xoxo LUV U

"Okay, so how much will this party cost?" my dad asked after he read my letter out loud for everyone in the kitchen to here.

"You're having a party?" Martin exclaimed in shock from the dining table.

"Yup! And guess what?" I snarked.

"What?"

"You're not invited!"

MY MIAMI 1992 - JANUARY (NEW YEAR, NEW DRAMA)

"We never said yes to this, Jennifer," my mom said as she peered at the letter.

"Please!" I begged. "I promise I will *never* ask you for anything else ever again. Dad, please make her say yes!"

"What's cost?" Dad asked again.

"I'm not sure yet," I admitted, "I haven't checked."

"Go check, we'll be here waiting for you," my mom said. She folded my note and put it aside on the table.

I walked to my room, called the community entertainment center for their rental prices, and totaled all the other costs. The overall price couldn't be *that* bad, right?

The cost $$$

Location: Community Entertainment Center

Number of attendees – 40

Party Duration – 3 hours

Room rental @ $50/hour - $150

Food for 40 people @ $15– $600

Goodie Bags for 25 kids – $125

Decorations – $200

MY MIAMI 1992 – JANUARY (NEW YEAR, NEW DRAMA)

Total - $1075

I almost screamed. There was no way my parents would spend anywhere near that amount of money for a birthday party. I stared at my list. There was no way my parents were going to say yes, but you never knew until you tried.

"*What*! Do you think I am made out of money!" my dad exclaimed when I revealed the costs. "That's like half the rent! Do you know how many things we could use that amount of money for?"

I regretted even saying anything.

"I said it would be *around* that price, so there may be a chance that it could be a lot less," I said, even though I knew it wasn't true.

"Honey, we can't afford something like that right now," my mom said, "Not even anything around that amount of money."

"Oh, come on! Dad, you pay for rent, and a car, and get paid every hour to sit in front of a computer. You're telling me you can't afford to pay for a little birthday party?" I whined.

"What you're planning to do here is definitely not a small birthday party," my dad remarked.

"Nor is it one we can afford," my mom added.

MY MIAMI 1992 - JANUARY (NEW YEAR, NEW DRAMA)

"This is so unfair. I've never had a birthday party before. Everyone at school has a party for their 13th. Even Martin ad one! Why can't I?" I complained. "It's not fair!"

"Life's not fair."

I stomped my foot on the ground, stormed up to my room, sat on my bed and pouted. I knew I that I was acting like an entitled brat, but I couldn't stop myself. Why couldn't I have what everyone else did?

My birthday party was supposed to my way of proving to the It Clique that I was fine without them, and that I have friends. Maybe I didn't have exactly 40 people I could call my friends, but I was determined to make them. I was going to prove what Skye had said about me wrong no matter what. Why couldn't I just have parents who cooperated with that?

I decided to divert my attention elsewhere... I began to think about things do besides from contemplate how my parents couldn't afford to throw 13th birthday party for me.

I ended up deciding to prepare what for Talia's birthday party that weekend. It was going to be the most exiting night of my life! I was going to meet Rayne Weaver! In the flesh! I had already formulated the thousands pf questions I was going to ask her for my research. Even if I didn't end up getting the chance to ask all my questions, I was going to find a way to get

MY MIAMI 1992 - JANUARY (NEW YEAR, NEW DRAMA)

her Louisiana address and maybe even phone number so I could contact her directly.

I needed to dress to impress, so I decided that I was going to wear my basic white silk dress, with black flats, and a fluffy blue sweater. I put on my outfit and went to the bathroom to see myself in the mirror. I was satisfied. I straightened my brown hair and completed the look by my dark blue sunglasses.

I looked at myself in the mirror one last time. I was ready.

MY MIAMI 1992 - JANUARY (NEW YEAR, NEW DRAMA)

Tuesday, January 21st, 1992

That day, during math class, Mr. Marshall gave us some free time, so I took it to my advantage and told Carolyn all about 13th birthday party plans. I made sure to leave out my motivations of gaining popularity and that my parents hadn't said yes because of the price. Carolyn seemed to be more excited than I was, which made me smile.

"That's so exiting Jennifer! Your birthday is in February, right? We have to plan this whole thing out, right now. It'll definitely be pink themed, with a huge cake, cupcake, balloons, and streamers. Also…"

My mind drifted as Carolyn went on talking about my party. I felt guilt creep up into as I thought about how I wasn't even convinced that the party was even happening. My parents hadn't even said yes. What if I didn't even end up having a party at all and got Carolyn all excited for nothing? Would she still want to be friends with me after that?

The bell rang, then Carolyn and I dashed towards the cafeteria to meet up with Florence and Lyla. Carolyn wanted to compile a guest list for the party while we ate.

Twenty minutes into lunch, the guest list was complete. It consisted of everyone I knew from school (most of which I barely spoke to), few friends from church, and family. Even though it would be impossible for me to invite everyone in the grade, I

MY MIAMI 1992 - JANUARY (NEW YEAR, NEW DRAMA)

wanted to invite people so that the party could be noticeable and talked about. The It Clique was only going to care or even notice if everyone spoke about it.

I grinned. It was going to be best party ever. The perfect revenge. If only I could find the means for it to happen… Was I getting everyone excited for nothing?

MY MIAMI 1992 - JANUARY (NEW YEAR, NEW DRAMA)

Wednesday, January 22nd, 1992

During English class, I admitted to Carolyn that my parents had turned down the idea of me having a 13th birthday party due to the cost. I had felt so guilty about getting everyone so excited that I had to come clean.

"Well to be fair, that is a lot of money," Carloyn said after I told her the truth, "Just be grateful you can even approach your parents when it comes to asking for that much. The minute I ask my mom for something over five dollars - Phew! She's flying out the window."

We both laughed. Parents could be so dramatic at times.

*****

After English class during our ten-minute break, I was in the middle of updating Florence and Lyla when Carolyn unexpectedly shifted the conversation.

"Ooo!" she squealed, "So you guys know how crazy I am for environmentalism and helping people right?"

"Yes," we all chorused at the same time.

"We should find a bunch of bottles, sell them at the bottle depot, then use the proceeds for Jennifer's birthday party," she went on. "We should make it a club… we'll call ourselves the Volunteer Squad!"

MY MIAMI 1992 - JANUARY (NEW YEAR, NEW DRAMA)

"That sounds so cool," Lyla said, tell us more.

Carolyn smiled at Lyla handed us a sheet of paper.

"These are my ideas so far," she said.

THE VOLUNTEER SQUAD!!!
A club where we help the elderly, the homeless, give donations, and just help out in the Grove. We can raise money for different events like a recycling fair, or things like that. We need at least 5 dedicated and committed members, and then we will get people to volunteer. We can do an audition. And then we can raise money for qualified student needs. We'll need parental involvement and sponsorship from the Students' Council. We'll make it an official school society, but first we need permission from the principal.

"What a great idea!" I exclaimed after we read it together. "That's a great way to raise money for my party!"

Carolyn raised an eyebrow at me but then shrugged it off. Why did she give me such a confused look? Didn't she just say it was to raise money for my birthday party?

"I'll have to talk to the principal about it after school," she said, "But I'll make sure to call you guys to let you know what she says."

*****

Carolyn, Lyla, Florence, and I were calmly eating our lunch in the cafeteria and

MY MIAMI 1992 - JANUARY (NEW YEAR, NEW DRAMA)

discussing what Carolyn was ought to say to the principal when Skye came up to us.

"Are you coming to Talia's party on Saturday?" she demanded.

I looked at Carolyn. She shook her head at me, indicating at me not to say anything. However, I knew that I couldn't, Skye had a master's degree in sabotage. I wasn't going to let her ruin my chances of meeting Rayne Weaver in person for me.

"No, why?" I lied.

"Good. Because she'd never want to invite someone like you anyway. She's our friend now, not yours."

Wow. Talia had officially joined the dark side. She was officially an It Clique member. I wondered how long it would take before they began to treat her the way they treated me.

Out of nowhere I began to laugh.

"What's so funny Chevrolet?" Skye snapped.

"Nothing," I immediately stopped laughing. I wasn't even sure what I found to be so funny in the situation.

"Okay Skye, are you done here?" Carolyn spoke up, waving her hand, "Nobody here cares about what you have to say."

"Whatever!" Skye scoffed. She looked me up and down, then walked away.

MY MIAMI 1992 – JANUARY (NEW YEAR, NEW DRAMA)

*****

When I came home that day, I pondered about the Volunteer Squad and how they may be able to raise funds for my party. It was only 5 weeks away and I was running out of time. I had decided to hold the celebration on Saturday, February 29th, since my birthday had fallen on a Wednesday.

I didn't believe that the Volunteer Squad would be able to get me enough money for the party through bottle drives, but it was my only option. There was no way they were going to be able to pay the full price, so we would have to attempt for at least half. Which was around five hundred dollars. I was going to have to beg my parents to pay the other portion.

"How about this, you pay for half of the party, and I'll pay for the other," I proposed to my parents in the living room.

My parents exchanged glances and told me that they still couldn't afford it. I became more irritated than I was the first time they said no. Why couldn't they just pay $500 and let me come up with the rest? Didn't they want me to celebrate officially becoming a teenager?

"Come on!" I whined, "I really, really, really, want this! Do you just not want me to have a birthday party then?!"

"We have nothing against you having a party," my dad said, "We just can't afford to pay for all the expenses right now."

MY MIAMI 1992 - JANUARY (NEW YEAR, NEW DRAMA)

I sighed. I felt a pang of guilt. My mom and dad were in a difficult financial situation and asking them for that amount of money was unreasonable.

I needed to lower the costs of my party.

The cost $$$

Location: Community Entertainment Center

~~Number of attendees - 40~~ 20 (GRRR!!!)

~~Party Duration - 3 hours~~ 2 hours

~~Renting a room for the party @ $50/hour - $150~~ $100

~~Food for 40 20 people @ $15 - $600~~ $300

~~Goodie Bags for 25 kids - $125~~

~~Decorations - $200~~ $100

New Total (UGH!) - 500$

I smiled as I looked at my list. Even though I wouldn't be able to invite as many people as I had anticipated, I would still be able to have fun at the party with small help from my parents and the Volunteer Squad.

Or so I thought, until...

MY MIAMI 1992 - JANUARY (NEW YEAR, NEW DRAMA)

Thursday, January 23rd, 1992

Lyla, Florence, and I waited in the courtyard before class that morning for Carolyn to share her news. She was going to let us know if the principal had approved her Volunteer Squad idea. Five minutes before the bell rang, Carolyn came dashing out of her mom's car with a huge poster in her hand.

"The principal said yes!" she shouted when she came up to us.

We all cheered. Carolyn showed us her Volunteer Squad poster, and I gasped, "This is amazing!"

"I spent all day yesterday working on it," she said.

"It looks awesome Carolyn, great job," Lyla said, then she turned to me, "Oh by the way Jennifer, how are your birthday party plans going?"

"My parents still said no!" I moaned.

"Now we just have to figure out how to raise all that money in such little time," Carolyn tapped her chin, "We'll have to be cutting costs... Or maybe you don't really have to have a big party. We could all have a slumber party!"

"Let's do the bottle drive idea; it would raise so much money." I suggested, ignoring Carolyn's suggestion, "I reduced the costs of the party already, so it shouldn't be too much of a hassle."

MY MIAMI 1992 - JANUARY (NEW YEAR, NEW DRAMA)

"I don't think we should keep that money for ourselves," Florence said quietly.

"But I need it for my party," I said looking at Carolyn for approval.

"Umm… I don't think that's how it works, Jen," Carolyn laughed while giving me a funny look.

She was staring at me as if I was crazy. Why wasn't she backing me up?

"But I thought the whole point of this club was to raise money to help throw my party," I said.

Carolyn folded her arms and looked at the ground. "You said so yesterday," I reminded her.

"Listen… I just don't think it's right for us to use fundraising money for a birthday party," Carolyn told me.

"So then what's the point of this club?" I asked.

"Umm… Hello!" Lyla cooed as she waved Carolyn's poster in my face. "To help make a better community at school and in the Grove?"

"Then how are we going to pay for my party?" I demanded, raising my voice.

"We can find another way, maybe a bake sale or lemonade stand," Carolyn suggested.

MY MIAMI 1992 - JANUARY (NEW YEAR, NEW DRAMA)

"You know what?" I said losing hope in the whole thing, "Just forget it."

Everyone stayed silent and stared at me.

I'd had enough of the conversation. I rushed into school as soon as the bell rang, not saying anything to any of them.

*****

For the rest of the day Carolyn and I didn't speak much. Even though I was mad her, I still agreed when Florence asked if I could help make a few fliers at home. It was the least I could do.

How was I going to make enough money for my party now? My parents still weren't willing to cover my unrealistic budget of $500 and the Volunteer Squad wasn't willing to help fundraise. How on earth was this going to work?

MY MIAMI 1992 - JANUARY (NEW YEAR, NEW DRAMA)

Friday, January 24th, 1992

I had instructed Martin the day before to get up early so that we could go to school early enough to give Carolyn the Volunteer Squad fliers. Unfortunately, my brother had slept in, making us both late to school.

Once I got to school, I dashed into the office to pick up a late slip. Students at Coconut Grove Academy were not allowed to sprint in the corridors, but I had a history class that morning, and my teacher despised tardiness.

After receiving my late slip, I went to my locker to put away my backpack, when I discovered a blue stick note slipped inside…

> *Hey Jennifer! It's me, your favorite person on earth, Talia! I just wanted to tell you to meet me in the seventh-grade girl's restroom immediately you see this, okay? Don't make me wait… Or else.*

Why did Talia always have a menacing tone in her voice whenever she spoke to me?! What on earth did Talia want to speak about? I didn't want to go because I assumed it would just be Meghan messing with me once again, but my curiosity got the best of me.

"Hey, I wanted to invite you to a cool hangout the girls and I are having," said Talia when I opened the restroom door.

"Girls?" I asked.

MY MIAMI 1992 - JANUARY (NEW YEAR, NEW DRAMA)

"Skye, Rosalyn, Emerald, and Charlotte - Meghan doesn't want to come, because I invited you."

"And Skye does?"

"I didn't tell her you were coming, just like I didn't tell her you're coming to my party tomorrow," Talia looked at herself in the mirror and played with her hair.

"Okay, but what are we going to do?" I asked. I wasn't going to agree to do just anything.

Talia looked at me, "Okay, okay, I know it sounds crazy to a bore like you, but-."

"Don't call me a bore," I said putting my hands on my hips, "If you brought me here just to insult me, I'm leaving."

Silence.

"Anyway!" she said sarcastically, not responding to my retort. "We were planning to sneak out on Sunday evening, to have a fun picnic together and watch the sunset."

"Yeah, no," I told her firmly, "I think the party invite was enough, I've never snuck out before anyway. I also don't plan to anytime soon."

Was she crazy? Sneaking out in the dark? At night?! Did she know how dangerous that was?

MY MIAMI 1992 - JANUARY (NEW YEAR, NEW DRAMA)

Talia laughed, "You've never snuck out before? Well, it's high time you experienced it! It's so fun!"

"Talia, we are a bunch of innocent twelve-year-old girls. We could easily get kidnapped, or worse."

"Oh, come on, Jennifer! Don't be a wimp. You have to go."

"I don't have to do anything… Why is it so important that I go anyway?"

"Well because I don't want to be alone with those girls."

"If you don't hate them so much, why are you even hanging out with them?!"

"That's none of your business, Chevrolet," she said, waving her hand dismissively at me.

"I just don't feel comfortable sneaking out. It's stupid anyway."

"Fine. If you don't want to come, don't expect to get a chance to meet my mom."

Wow.

I couldn't believe Talia was using her party to manipulate me. It was pure evil! I needed to get into contact with Rayne Weaver, and even though Talia probably didn't know why, she was clearly aware that I desperate and was using it against me. Why did people have to be like this?

MY MIAMI 1992 - JANUARY (NEW YEAR, NEW DRAMA)

"Just say yes," Talia laughed, while interrupting my thoughts.

"Talia, you're not being fair," I told her.

"Welp," she said as she patted me on the shoulder, "Life's not fair. Get used to it, Chevrolet."

Talia walked out of the restroom and peeked her head back inside, "You have until tomorrow to let me know by the way."

What was I going to do?!

*****

I was desperate to meet Rayne Weaver. I *had* to meet her. I was certain that if I got to interview her, I would have a better chance of winning the Project Author's challenge, which would allow me to assist my family in putting money towards a mortgage to move into a nicer home. I had to win the first-place 10,00$ prize for my parents. I owed it to them.

Talia's main plan was for us to "sneak out," but I thought it was silly and dangerous. So instead, I made a better plan. I would ask my mom to go, and with her permission, I would attend but lie to Talia and tell her that I slipped away. That way, no one would be harmed.

"Absolutely not," my mother hissed when I asked.

"Mom! Please! It's just a picnic!" I whined.

MY MIAMI 1992 - JANUARY (NEW YEAR, NEW DRAMA)

"Besides, aren't you going to this party tomorrow? Yeah, so no."

"But mom!"

"If you ask me one more time, you're not going to that birthday party."

I went upstairs to my room without a word. All I was getting from my parents the past few days were no's, no's, and more no's. I was fed up.

The more I thought about the sneak-out plan, the less it seemed like such a horrendous idea. Don't get me wrong: I disliked the fact that we were going to be defying our parents, but it wasn't like we were going to a nightclub or anything. It was just a harmless beach picnic; yeah, it was with some of the world's most heinous people, but it wasn't like we were doing anything illegal.

I needed to meet Rayne Weaver for the welfare of my family. I knew that Talia was manipulating me, but it didn't matter because I *had* to do it. I wanted to help my struggling parents to buy their dream home in the suburbs, I owed it to them.

I had to do it. Even if I was going to get caught, it was all going to be worth it in the end.

I remembered the time when Martin snuck away to one of his friend's parties when he was sixteen. My dad was enraged; I had never seen him so angry before. He grounded

MY MIAMI 1992 - JANUARY (NEW YEAR, NEW DRAMA)

Martin for a month and assigned him several extra chores. If I got it was going to be horrible, but what other option did I have?

Talia was overjoyed when I called to inform her that I was coming to the picnic. She also let me know that her mother had arrived in Miami earlier that morning and was staying in a hotel. It was confirmed, she was going to be there.

Suddenly all my worries about the Sunday sneak out were flushed out by my excitement. I was finally going to meet Rayne Weaver! It was going to be the best day of my life.

MY MIAMI 1992 - JANUARY (NEW YEAR, NEW DRAMA)

Saturday, January 25th, 1992

Briiiiinnnggg! That morning, I awoke with a huge load of energy. It was eight o'clock in the morning, a rare time for someone like me to be awake on a Saturday morning. However, it wasn't just a regular Saturday… It was the Saturday where I was going to meet the key to my success – Rayne Weaver!

I was ecstatic to meet Rayne Weaver, but I hated the price that I would have to pay for it. It was so stupid, but I knew that I had no other choice.

Since the day I was born, my family and I had been living in our cramped three-bedroom condo. We all hated it. My parents spoke about owning their own home in the suburbs daily. We always drove around the suburbs of the Grove looking at houses, discussing which ones we preferred and why. If I could win the Project Author's contest, all the money would go to my family. We needed it.

*****

It was finally time for the party, and I was a nervous wreck! The supposed to be a twenty-minute car ride to Talia's place felt like 20 hours, with the typical hectic Miami traffic.

I persisted in urging my dad to drive faster until he finally got fed up and said, "Are you trying to get me a speeding ticket?! Because if I do, you will be the one paying for it."

MY MIAMI 1992 – JANUARY (NEW YEAR, NEW DRAMA)

So, I gave up and watched my dad drive in solitude. Why couldn't everyone just move faster?

We eventually arrived in one piece and right on time. Talia's house was an acreage just outside the Grove. The house was large and spacious with about 4000 square feet of living space and a large hall where guests were entertained. The music boomed through speakers. Meghan's place was nothing compared to Talia's. It appeared as though everyone who walked into the Coconut Grove Academy was filthy rich… Except for my family of course.

Talia's house was packed; with people from school and people that I had never seen before. It was an insane, trendy, 90's style, high school level party. It was by far one of the coolest parties that I had ever been to.

Talia had just moved into the Grove. How did she know so many people? Were all these people invited by her or the It Clique? There was no way Talia could build up that much popularity within only a month at her new school. However, I thought, she was hanging out with five of the most popular girls at the school, so it must not have been too difficult.

Suddenly I began to think of Meghan. I thought of how she was going to react to me being invited to such an epic party. Part of me was excited to see her reaction and the other was nervous. All I knew was that she was not going to be happy.

MY MIAMI 1992 - JANUARY (NEW YEAR, NEW DRAMA)

I waited for Carolyn to arrive in Talia's den. I had only seen Talia a few times in passing and I hadn't gotten the chance to wish her happy birthday and present her gift. So, I decided to just place my gift alongside the large pile of others in the corner. Even though my gift was small compared to others, I hoped that Talia would like it. I had gotten her some cute bath bombs, pens, a notebook, and a card with a note saying:

Happy Birthday, Talia! I hope 13 treats you well and that you have an amazing day!

- Jennifer :)

I stared at the large pile of presents. My tiny gift bag was nothing compared to the others. I then began to wonder what type of presents I would receive if I threw my own party…

I was about to get up from the couch to go fetch some chips when I noticed Emerald and Rosalyn stroll by. I instantly went into hiding. I wasn't ready for the It Clique to know that I was there yet.

I decided to go to the basement. Most of the party was taking place upstairs in the kitchen and den, so there weren't many people in the basement. It was a much calmer environment than all the business downstairs. I sat on a chair, ate the rest of my pizza, and watched the movie that was playing on the TV.

MY MIAMI 1992 - JANUARY (NEW YEAR, NEW DRAMA)

Twenty minutes later, Carolyn entered the basement looking for me.

"Hey Jen!" Carolyn called when she saw me, "What are you doing in here? All the fun's upstairs."

"Nothing, just hiding from the It Clique," I laughed.

Carolyn smiled at me and shook her head. "It was so nice of Talia to invite us! Despite being friends with Meghan and all, she seems like such a nice girl."

"Yeah, I wish," I muttered under my breath thinking about the sneak-out.

"I wish Florence and Lyla could have come," Carolyn went on, "This house is huge, her parents must be loaded."

"Yeah, well, her mom's a well-known author," I reminded her.

Carolyn was already aware of my desire to meet Rayne Weaver. The only thing she wasn't aware of was my desire to compete in the Project Author's challenge. Even though I knew I could trust Carolyn, I decided not to tell her just in case. After the Meghan situation, I was sure to be extra careful of who I told things to.

"Her Dad's also a real estate agent. He owns a bunch of buildings around the city, even the building a block away from mine," Carolyn added. "Lyla told me yesterday."

MY MIAMI 1992 - JANUARY (NEW YEAR, NEW DRAMA)

"That's not true," I laughed, thinking of when Talia said her dad was a teacher. "Her Dad's a teacher, she said so on the first day of school. Remember?"

"She was probably just lying to be humble or something," Carolyn told me, "You know the TW MAX real estate company?"

"Yeah."

"That's her dad's company. It was named after Talia, Talia Weaver Max Real Estate."

I was taken aback. Why would Talia lie about that?! It didn't make sense to me why someone would conceal the fact that their parents were rich. What was so shameful about having a dad who owned five percent of the buildings in town?

Even though Talia's lies had me perplexed, the exhilaration of meeting Rayne Weaver obscured my bewilderment. Carolyn and I had planned to spend the entire party in the basement until Rayne Weaver arrived. However, once we overheard people discussing more pizza arriving, we couldn't resist heading upstairs to get some more slices.

Carolyn and I discreetly went upstairs and waited quietly for Meghan and her squad to leave the kitchen, then went inside Talia's kitchen and grabbed our slices. We were just about to return to the basement when Talia appeared out of nowhere.

MY MIAMI 1992 – JANUARY (NEW YEAR, NEW DRAMA)

"Hi Talia! Happy birthday!" I said before she could say anything. "Thank you so much for inviting me."

"You're going to pay me back for it anyway, so…" Talia looked Carolyn up and down. "You're welcome too."

Carolyn gave me a funny look, then gave Talia another, "Thanks, I left your present with the rest of them," she answered nonchalantly.

Talia nodded then looked at me, "So, how are you enjoying the party so far?"

"It's pretty good," I replied, "There's a whole lot of people here."

"Yeah, Meghan wanted me to have a good amount of people, so – here we are!" she said, scanning the room with her hands on her hips.

"So, you listen to Meghan's orders now?" I laughed at her.

"It's just super frustrating since if my dad finds out I'm having this party without any adults he'll kill me," Talia said randomly without answering my question.

"What?!" Carolyn and I both exclaimed in shock.

Talia smirked at me, "Oh? You didn't know? I told my dad that my mom would be supervising the party, and I told my mom that my dad would be. They don't talk ever so it doesn't really matter."

MY MIAMI 1992 - JANUARY (NEW YEAR, NEW DRAMA)

"Wow!" Carolyn exclaimed.

"So that means your mom's not going to come?"

"Oh, she's going to come, but just for a little while to give me a present and pick up her letters. You can talk to her while she's doing all that," Talia said. "Besides, what's a cool party when parents are around?"

"Talia, once my mom and Dad find out I went to a party without parental supervision they are going to be so mad," I scolded her.

"Agreed," Carolyn chimed.

Talia looked at Carolyn up and down, and there was an awkward silence.

It made sense why Talia's house was so packed and rowdy. There were absolutely no parents around to make sure the kids were safe. This was crazy!

Talia was about to say something when someone bumped into me and got soda all over my beloved white dress.

"Caleb!" Carolyn exclaimed, "What is wrong with you!?"

The boy quickly meaninglessly apologized, offered me some paper towels, and walked away. Boys.

MY MIAMI 1992 – JANUARY (NEW YEAR, NEW DRAMA)

Carolyn and Talia were helping me clean up when a voice I recognized like the back of my hand said, "Umm... Excuse me?! What is *she* doing here?!"

I turned around to see Meghan with her hands on her hips and the It Clique standing behind her. Carolyn's shouting at the guy who ruined my dress must have caught their attention. Great.

Meghan walked up to Talia, "Talia! I have told you how many times. I do not want to be anywhere she is."

"Yeah!" Skye called on.

"Shut up, Skye! I told you to ask Jennifer if she was invited and you said no. You knew she was going to be here," Meghan barked at her suddenly.

Carolyn and I looked at each other in disbelief. Neither of us had ever heard Meghan talk to Skye like that before. It was unbelievable to me how big of a fuss Meghan was making over me being invited to birthday party.

"But she –," Skye was about to say.

"Don't say another word," Meghan said to her dangerously.

Who in the world did Meghan think she was? It was Talia's party, not hers. She had no right to decide who was invited or not. It didn't make any sense to me why Talia was standing there taking all the insults.

MY MIAMI 1992 - JANUARY (NEW YEAR, NEW DRAMA)

At that point Meghan was speaking loud enough that people were starting to pay attention to the conversation. I did *not* want this to happen.

"And why are you talking to her, Talia? If you want to be a part of us, you can't speak to or hang out with ex-members. I've told you this!" Meghan shouted.

I almost laughed. Meghan was dictatorial that it didn't make sense to me why anyone would want to be friends with her.

I looked over at Talia. Was she just going to let Meghan bark at her like that?

"You're not the boss of her, Meghan," Carolyn said suddenly. She had a cool and calm tone in her voice, "You're not the boss of anyone."

Uh-oh. I watched in fear as Meghan's eye's switched from Talia to Carolyn.

"What did you just say?" Meghan asked dangerously.

"I said, you're not the boss of anyone, Meghan," Carolyn repeated with an antagonizing smile.

Meghan's face turned hot red. I couldn't believe that Carolyn was able to take Meghan Benjaminson's power and deflate her ego. She challenged her authority in a way that no one had ever done before.

As Carolyn and Meghan continued to stare at each other I realized something. It was my

MY MIAMI 1992 – JANUARY (NEW YEAR, NEW DRAMA)

battle not hers. She didn't have to single-handedly stand up for me; I had to do it for myself.

"Meghan," I spoke up, "Leave her alone."

"Jennifer don't speak to me," Meghan fired back.

"I can do and speak to whoever I want. You are not in charge of me. This is not your house, neither is it your party - it's Talia's. So, Talia has the right to invite anyone she wants. Got it?"

I wasn't even sure why I chose to defend Talia. She could have easily done it herself.

I was astonished as everyone jeered at Meghan. I watched her face turn from hot red to a bright pink. Finally, Meghan Benjaminson was taken off from her high horse. Even though it was for Talia, standing up to her was the best feeling ever.

I had never seen Meghan look so embarrassed and angry in my life. She looked as if she wanted to explode.

"This isn't over, Jennifer," she told me. "You may have won the battle, but you haven't won the war."

The battle line had been drawn.

I looked over at Talia. She rolled her eyes and shook her head. Not a single word had left her mouth.

MY MIAMI 1992 - JANUARY (NEW YEAR, NEW DRAMA)

Meghan turned to the It Clique, "Listen. I'm leaving this party, so you better come along with me unless you want to become the next Chevrolet."

The girls scrambled all over the place looking for their things. Then with a final happy birthday and a slam of the door, the It Clique left.

*****

I was annoyed. It had been an hour since the It Clique had left, my white dress was still stained, and Talia's mom still hadn't arrived. I was on my way to confront Talia when I heard a ring on the doorbell that caught my attention.

I watched as Talia walked over and opened the door…

I stared as the door opened. It felt as though had stopped as I watched a woman walk inside… Rayne Weaver.

Talia was engulfed into a tight hug. It surreal seeing Rayne Weaver in the flesh. She was holding a massive cake carton and gift bag in her hands.

I signaled for Carolyn – who was sitting in the den – to come over.

"Oh my gosh! Oh my gosh! Oh my gosh! It's Rayne Weaver!" I squealed when she walked over to me.

MY MIAMI 1992 – JANUARY (NEW YEAR, NEW DRAMA)

"I know, I know!" Carolyn jumped up and down reflecting my excitement.

Talia introduced her mom to the group. After cutting the cake and singing "Happy Birthday," to Talia, I finally took my shot to talk to Rayne Weaver.

"Hi Ms. Weaver," I waved, walking up to her. She was eating her cake alone at the counter while the kids partied. She looked up at me and Carolyn.

I then realized I was supposed to call her Ms. Benjaminson, not Weaver anymore. Shoot.

"I - I must say – I'm such a huge fan of your books!" I stuttered. Come on Jennifer, talk! "I've read almost all of them! They're the best! You are such an inspiration to me, and I've been dying to meet you."

Ugh! Why couldn't I just act normal?

Ms. Benjaminson thanked me and laughed. I then went on to bravely ask if I could ask her a few questions about herself. I crossed my hands behind my back in hopes that she would say yes.

Fortunately, she did and invited Carolyn and I to sit down with her. My heart raced as Carolyn and I grabbed chairs and sat across from her. I couldn't believe that I was speaking with Rayne Weaver!

I asked her a few basic questions about her life and told her about how she inspired my passion for writing. I made it a point to mention that I had been sending her letters for nearly two weeks with no response.

"Yes, I am so sorry about that. I actually came by to pick those letters up," she apologized, "I'll give you my personal address and phone number, so you can send me letters or call directly."

I beamed. My hero was giving me her address and phone number to connect with her anytime! Suddenly, everything I had worked for the past weeks began to feel worth it.

"Thank you so much, Ms. Benjaminson!" I said.

"Oh, please call me Rayne - Rayne Benjaminson!"

"Okay, Rayne!" Carolyn laughed in response.

Even though Rayne Weaver - Benjaminson - had granted us permission, it felt strange to call her "Rayne". I had always been told that calling adults by their first name was impolite, so I decided to just stick with Ms. Benjaminson.

When Ms. Benjaminson walked away to get some snacks, I looked at Carolyn and gave her a hug.

"Can you believe that just happened?!" I squealed.

"I know! All your hard work paid off! You worked so hard for this, you really deserve it, Jen!" Carolyn congratulated me.

I stared at the sticky note Ms. Benjaminson had given me.

Phone: 888 182 7809

2848 67th Street (Unit 28)

[illegible]

I clutched the piece of paper in my hands and promised myself to never lose it. I made sure to also rewrite it down in my notebook once I got home, just in case.

I was super exhilarated that I had met Rayne Weaver, but I was in a nervous wreck for the price that I had to pay in exchange... Defy my parents and sneak out of the house.

This was going to go so wrong.

MY MIAMI 1992 - JANUARY (NEW YEAR, NEW DRAMA)

Sunday, January 26th, 1992

I was going to get caught. I just knew it. I could have just bailed out of the plan, by saying that I was sick or something, but Talia would still figure out how to force me into doing something even worse. It was stupid, but did I have any other choice?

We were going to have our picnic at the famous South Beach; I made sure to bring a few snacks, in case the girls decided they wanted to be stingy and not let me have anything. I didn't trust anyone in the It Clique, so I wasn't going to take my chances. I never wanted to hang out with people like them ever again.

I became ten times more nervous when it finally was time to get on the bus and head over to the beach. My mom and dad were away at a church program, so it was easy to leave home. Martin was supposed to be watching me, but he was busy taking a nap in his room. There was no way he was going to notice me slipping away.

I hated the fact that I was leaving without anyone knowing where I would be, where I was going. What if I got lost while taking the bus? The South Beach was a twenty-five-minute-long drive away from my house, so it would take forever for someone to find me.

I was going to make sure that I would only spend one hour at the beach and then return home, whether they had arrangements for me to get a ride back home or not. My parents weren't going to be home until 8:00 PM that night so it was crucial for me to be at

MY MIAMI 1992 - JANUARY (NEW YEAR, NEW DRAMA)

home before then. Once I got home, I planned to bribe Martin with some of my allowance money so he wouldn't tell. Simple. I was not going to let anyone mess it up for me.

I walked to the bus stop a couple blocks away from my house. I waited patiently but also nervously as I wanted for the South Beach express bus to arrive.

I had taken the Miami Dade transportation many times before, but never alone. I was petrified. Once the bus arrived, I took a good look at the driver who smiled, then decided to sit at the front to feel safer.

I finally arrived at the beach when the sun was slowly starting to set. Surprisingly, there wasn't a huge crowd, so it wasn't that difficult for me to spot the It Clique.

"Wow! About time you showed up!" Talia laughed when she saw me, "I thought you would chicken out."

I looked at the uncompleted It Clique Meghan, Emerald, and Skye weren't there. I wasn't surprised by Meghan's lack of attendance since Talia had told me earlier that she wasn't going to be there.

"Where are the other two?" I asked.

"Meghan called each of us this morning and told us that we couldn't go and of course Skye obeyed," Charlotte said with an annoyed tone, "Emerald never planned to come from the get-go."

MY MIAMI 1992 - JANUARY (NEW YEAR, NEW DRAMA)

"And you guys disobeyed?" I asked in disbelief.

Wow. Rebellion in the It Clique? That was unheard of!

"Meghan was being so rude to us yesterday, whereas Talia was the one who invited you," Rosalyn said looking at Talia, "I don't get why she's mad at us. It was Talia's fault, not ours."

"Meghan kicked Emerald out of the It Clique for a week," Talia said, ignoring Rosalyn's comment. "She and Meghan got in a brawl yesterday about leaving my party early."

"She's so bossy," Charlotte groaned, "I bet Emerald doesn't even like her. And to be honest right now, I don't either."

I couldn't believe how much tea about the It Clique the girls were spilling to me – an outsider. I thought they all hated me. I knew that Meghan and Skye did, but did that mean everyone else in the crew did?

"You can't tell Meghan we are saying this by the way," Rosalyn told me, "Or that we even came here."

"Yeah! Honestly Jennifer, ever since you left, Meghan has been acting so different," Charlotte told me, "She's always on edge."

I couldn't believe what Rosalyn and Charlotte were saying about Meghan. I then began to wonder what Skye would have if she was there. She would have said anything to defend Meghan. Skye was loyal to Meghan, the same way I was when I was in the It Clique.

I looked at Talia, and as expected she stayed quiet. She was smart, but in a mischievous and uncanny way. You never knew what she was thinking.

"To be honest," Talia spoke up out of nowhere. "I think with Emerald getting kicked out, Meghan will probably end up replacing her with someone else."

Then Talia dismissed herself and began to pace herself towards the public restrooms.

"Ugh, I hate her!" Charlotte muttered when Talia walked away, "But Meghan loves her, so I have to keep quiet."

"I really don't think she's that bad," Rosalyn told Charlotte. "She's just… mysterious."

I couldn't believe Rosalyn and Charlotte went from ranting about Meghan to talking about Talia in the span of a few seconds. They were such gossips.

"She's so - weird! You just can't figure out who's side she's on," Charlotte told me, "Nobody knows anything about her, not even Rosalyn, and she knows everything about everyone."

Then Charlotte whispered something into Rosalyn's ear.

MY MIAMI 1992 - JANUARY (NEW YEAR, NEW DRAMA)

"Jennifer. Tell anyone about what we just said, I promise I will make you regret it. Okay?" Charlotte warned, placing her dark brown eyes into the depths of my soul.

I nodded. I had no intention of saying anything at all. I didn't want to be involved in any drama involving the It Clique what's so ever.

Once Talia came back, the sunset had officially begun, and we watched in silence. It wasn't as fun as hanging out with Carolyn, Lyla, and Florence, but it was fun to watch nature at work. A little part of me missed hanging out with the It Clique, but I knew it would never happen again. Things were just too different now.

"Wow, so you're really not hanging out with us anymore, huh?" Charlotte said, breaking the silence.

"Yeah, well Meghan kicked me out, so I guess not," I replied, still staring at the sky.

"So, you're never coming back?" Rosalyn asked curiously.

"No... No, most definitely not. I have better friends now and they make me feel appreciated and like a better person," I shrugged, "I was a mess when I hung out with you guys."

No one responded to my calling my new friends "better".

MY MIAMI 1992 - JANUARY (NEW YEAR, NEW DRAMA)

No matter what, I was never going back ot the It Clique. Even if I had the smallest feeling that the girls missed me. They were just going to have to deal with it. My association with Meghan, Talia, Skye, Emerald, Charlotte, and Rosalyn was going to be terminated immediately after the picnic.

"What do you think do you think about this entire situation," I asked Talia. I wanted to hear her pure thoughts, since I was unclear what of what they were.

Talia looked at me and smiled, "All is fair in love and war, Jennifer."

What did that even mean?

"What does that have to do with anything! You've been silent the whole time, no one can get a read on you, Talia!"

"You'll see, you'll see," Talia laughed.

Suddenly, we heard a stern male voice behind us, "Excuse me ladies? What are you doing here by yourself? Where are your parents?"

We turned around to see a police officer hovering over us, with a stern look on his face. We were busted.

"They're in the parking lot," Talia lied.

"Okay, take me to them," he said. "You should not be here alone. How old are you?"

MY MIAMI 1992 – JANUARY (NEW YEAR, NEW DRAMA)

I took a deep breath. "Don't panic, Jennifer," I told myself.

"I'm 12," I said to the officer quickly.

"Me too," Rosalyn said. She then pointed to Charlotte, "She's 13."

"I'm 16," Talia lied again.

"She's actually 13," I said glaring at her. Why in the world was she lying to a police officer?

We were already in big enough trouble, and I wasn't going to let Talia get us into more. I was not going to put myself into trouble by lying to a police officer. Talia had crossed the line.

"We snuck out," I said without hesitation.

"I didn't," Rosalyn said, looking at me with confusion. "My mom dropped me off, and one of my sisters, Sophie, is going to pick us up."

"Me too," Charlotte said. "You can call our parents to confirm if you'd like."

I was stunned. I thought the whole idea of Sunday Sneak Out was for us *all* to sneak out of our houses and go the beach? Talia lied to me! How could she? Why did was only me who had to sneak out and nobody else? I was furious.

"Talia, did you sneak out?" Charlotte asked her.

MY MIAMI 1992 – JANUARY (NEW YEAR, NEW DRAMA)

"Yeah," she admitted.

The police officer took our names and when he heard mine, he paused.

"Jennifer? As in Jennifer Alexis Chevrolet?" He asked me urgently.

I looked back at the girls, and they all shrugged, "Um... Yes?"

What was going on? How did the officer already know my name?

"The police have been looking all over town for you. Who would have known you were at South Beach?" the man told me.

He made a phone call on his speaker to let another officer know that I was safe and at South Beach. He then told us that he would explain everything once he dropped us all off at our mess.

I couldn't believe it. Martin had called the police when he found out I wasn't at home. I was finished.

*****

It was the scariest car ride of my life. I was being driven home in a cop-car and had to face my parents. Once we arrived at my house, I glared at Talia one last time and hopped out of the vehicle. Talia and I were going to have a *huge* talk when we saw each other again.

The cop came out of the vehicle, walked me to the door of my house, and knocked the

MY MIAMI 1992 - JANUARY (NEW YEAR, NEW DRAMA)

door. I was almost terrified to see my parents.

"Where were you?" my dad's voice boomed when he opened the door.

Then the angry look on his face turned into horror when he saw the cop. Then my mom came over and carried the same expression. I looked at their faces and felt so ashamed of myself.

"Officer?" my dad asked.

"Look who I found!" the officer replied. He said it almost as if it was funny. It wasn't. At all.

He then explained the situation.

"Apparently," he said, "She had snuck out to hang out with three other friends at Soth Beach. I'm dropping everyone off and having a chat with their parents. Everyone will be at home safe in no time."

"Oh, my goodness! Thank you, Officer! Thank you!" my parents echoed.

"All good. Now, Jennifer, be a good girl, and no more sneaking out and scaring our parents. Okay? It's a dark world out there, so it's important be careful," the officer said to me.

I was tongue-tied, but I nodded.

The officer made his final notes in his notebook, chatted a little bit more with

MY MIAMI 1992 - JANUARY (NEW YEAR, NEW DRAMA)

parents, and then left me alone to face the dire consequences of my actions.

I watched as the police officer walked out the door. I wanted to join him wherever he was going. The last thing I wanted at that moment was to be left alone to face my parents. I wanted to disappear.

"You snuck out?" I had never seen my dad look so furious in his life.

"Do you know what you just put us through? Sneaking out? Jennifer, what has gotten into you?" my mom cried.

"I'm sorry -," I began.

"Keep quiet, young lady!" my dad snapped. "Go sit in the corner and face the wall!"

"What?"

"I said, in the corner!"

"But Dad, I -."

"I said keep quiet! Because you don't know what I want to do with you right now!" he yelled.

Fear ran through my bones. My dad was yelling so loud that I was afraid our neighbors would hear and call the police on a father gone crazy.

For twenty minutes straight, I was in the corner of the living room, with my dad lecturing and yelling at me. Tears rolled down my cheeks the entire time.

MY MIAMI 1992 - JANUARY (NEW YEAR, NEW DRAMA)

Once Dad calmed down a little, my mom sat me down and asked exactly where I was, who I was with, and why I had snuck out in the first place. I reminded my mom about how I had previously asked to go but she said no. She recalled the conversation but could not believe I followed through with it after our discussion. She was disappointed in me.

My mom sent me up to my room and told me that she would be discussing my punishment with my dad. They were going to let me know what it was the following morning.

I wanted to blame someone for the mess I had gotten into. I wanted to blame Talia, Meghan, or even Skye, but I knew I couldn't. It was my fault. I made the choice to fall into Talia's manipulation and defy my parents. It was all on me. I deserved whatever punishment I was given. I should have never done it in the first place. There were probably easier ways to get connected to Rayne Weaver, yet I was impatient and desperate, and of course, my desperation led to me making foolish choices.

I had lost my parents' trust, all because I lacked a backbone. I had decided to take part in the Author's Project challenge because I wanted to impress my parents. I wanted to make them proud, but instead of doing that I disappointed them.

I fell asleep that night in tears and shame.

MY MIAMI 1992 - JANUARY (NEW YEAR, NEW DRAMA)

Monday, January 27th, 2021

I woke up that morning with red eyes, a terrible headache, and my ears still ringing from my dad yelling the previous night. I felt terrible, yet my mom still forced me to go to school.

Great.

I was grounded "for life" - no electronics, no tv, and no going out with friends. Fantastic!

Once I arrived at school, Carolyn, Lyla, and Florence – the Volunteer Squad - ran up to me urgently.

"Oh my gosh! Jennifer, are you okay?" Carolyn exclaimed, "I heard what happened yesterday! I called you a million times, your parents kept saying you were unavailable. What happened? Everyone in school is talking about it!"

I said nothing. I didn't understand why everyone was making a such big deal out of the whole thing. We simply got a ride home in a police car and were escorted home. Simple.

Carolyn kept on begging me to tell her what had happened, but I kept on changing the subject. I didn't want to talk or even think about what had happened on Sunday. All I cared about that day was seeing Talia so we could have a talk.

*****

MY MIAMI 1992 - JANUARY (NEW YEAR, NEW DRAMA)

That day, I didn't see Talia anywhere. She was so lucky. I had already prepared what I was going to say when I saw her and it wasn't going to be pretty.

"Oh my gosh! Did you hear?" Lyla exclaimed when I got to our lunch table, "Just now. As we speak! Meghan just announced that she's kicking Rosalyn out of the group."

"What!" I was shocked.

"Well apparently, Talia told Meghan that Rosalyn forced her and Charlotte to go to South Beach and threatened to spread rumors about them if they didn't."

"What? That is *not* true. They didn't even sneak out. It wasn't even Rosalyn's idea!" I exclaimed in utter disbelief.

Talia had a plan. I wasn't sure what it was at that moment, but she had a mission and was strategically executing it. It was like a game of chess. The school was Talia's chess board, and the members of the It Clique her pawns. I then began to wonder what my role was in Talia's games.

"So, what's going on with the Volunteer Squad?" I asked trying to change the subject.

"Well, we haven't got an exact date on when we will hold our first meeting, but we know it's going to be sometime next month," Florence said. "The executive members will be you, Carolyn, Lyla, and me, but we still need one more person."

MY MIAMI 1992 - JANUARY (NEW YEAR, NEW DRAMA)

"And Lyla had this amazing idea for an event we could do." Carolyn added. "An event where we gather a bunch of students to volunteer to help clean the South Beach! I'm sure we'll find lots of bottles, sell them, and use the funds to donate towards a charity of our choice."

Ugh. I did not want to return to South Beach after what had happened on the previous day. I never wanted to go to that beach ever again.

"Also, Jen, how are the birthday party plans coming up?" Carolyn asked curiously.

I hadn't even thought of mt birthday party yet. After what had happened, there was probably a one to zero percent chance of my party happening.

"Pretty good," I lied.

I didn't want to think about my party. I didn't want to think about anything that revolved around me. I wanted to focus on my grades, friends, and family. It was time for me to put others above myself.

MY MIAMI 1992 - JANUARY (NEW YEAR, NEW DRAMA)

Tuesday, January 28th, 1992

People at school were still talking about what had happened on Sunday. I wanted to explode. There were so many false rumors being, making my friends - specifically Carolyn - question me about it every five seconds. wouldn't stop asking me about it. Why did the It Clique have to be so popular?

At lunch Carolyn, Florence, and I were sitting at our table eating lunch Lyla came running up to us.

"Guys! Guess what?" Lyla said when she sat down next to me, across from Carolyn and Florence.

On most days, I sat beside Carolyn, with Florence and Lyla across from us. However, things were starting to get a bit tense between Carolyn and I since I refused to talk about the Sunday Sneak Out.

"What?" I asked.

"You know how I told you how my mom works as secretary at the Coconut Grove Country Club?" Lyla said.

"Yeah, continue," Carolyn's eyes flickered with excitement.

"Well recently there has been some shortage of staff, because a bunch of staff quit at the last minute," Lyla said.

"Why?"

MY MIAMI 1992 - JANUARY (NEW YEAR, NEW DRAMA)

"I don't know exactly. Something to do with the vice-president of the club stealing a bunch of money… Either way, I told her about the Volunteer Squad, and she talked to the president about it. He said that we can volunteer to teach a few of the kids' classes!" she said.

"Oh my gosh, that sounds so cool!" Florence exclaimed, "How long will they be needing us to volunteer?"

"She says until the end of February or March to give them time to find some new staff," Lyla answered.

She took a folded paper out of her pocket. "Here's the sign-up sheet."

Volunteer Sign Up Sheets

Level 2 Swimming Lessons – *Caleb Miller*
Introductory Level Horse Back Riding Class - Lyla Williams
Little Kids Soccer Training -
Breakfast Cooking Class -
Creative Movement Class -

I didn't think that it was a good idea. All the volunteering opportunities looked time consuming. I wanted to calmly turn it down, but I knew that it would make Carolyn upset. I could tell she didn't believe I was dedicated to the Volunteer Squad. I was going to prove to her that I was.

"This is perfect," Carolyn said while clapping her hands together. "We can even do the beach cleanup and save the money in our treasurer or something."

MY MIAMI 1992 - JANUARY (NEW YEAR, NEW DRAMA)

"Okay, which one do you guys want to do?" Lyla said while looking at her list.

"I'll do the cooking class," Carolyn said. "I cook all the time and taking it as one of my electives."

"I'll do soccer, my little brother trains there, so I'll get to spend more time with him," Florence said. "I'm also on the girls' soccer team, so I have a lot of experience."

"Well, I guess that leaves me with the Creative Movement class," I shrugged.

I was not excited, but I pretended as if I was. Spending the next one or two months teaching kids how to dance did not sound like any fun.

"Adrienne Miller, the volunteer supervisor, will be supervising us the whole time, so we have to be on our A game," Lyla warned us. "Also, whenever you can, stay away from Mr. & Mrs. Miller."

"Why?" I asked curiously.

"Let's just say they're like the It Clique of the country club. Mr. Miller is vice president of the club, and Mrs. Miller is chairperson of the social committee. Lots of staff have been complaining about them recently," Lyla explained. "Their daughter Adrienne is nice, she's seventeen, but just don't get yourself involved because she can unpredictable. The Millers have a son too, his name is..."

MY MIAMI 1992 - JANUARY (NEW YEAR, NEW DRAMA)

My mind wandered as the girls kept talking about the country club and the Miller's family. When the bell rang, I quickly got out of my seat, said goodbye, and headed straight to math class.

Lately, I hadn't been doing very well in math my math class. I usually an A-student, so when I got a B- on my last exam, I was concerned. What if my B- turned into a C+?

I needed to get an A on my math exam that Friday. Maybe if I had gotten a good mark, I could use it as a leeway into convincing my parents to let me have a 13th birthday party.

I needed to put more focus into my schoolwork. I had been so focused on finding Rayne Benjaminson, I had slacked in my academics, and it was showing in my grades. I needed to get my head back in the game.

MY MIAMI 1992 - JANUARY (NEW YEAR, NEW DRAMA)

Wednesday, January 29th, 1992

I woke up extra early that morning to finish my science homework. I was so busy studying for my math exam the night before that I had fallen asleep before I could complete it.

When I got to school, I was exhausted. I was digging in my locker looking for my calculator when Talia walked up behind me.

"So, I heard you're going to start volunteering at country club," Talia laughed. "Sounds pretty rich kid like to me."

"Look who's talking," I told her. A part of me wanted how she even knew about that, but I knew better.

I had already decided that I wasn't going to talk to Talia anymore, but I still wanted to confront about what happened on Sunday. She wasn't going to off that easy.

"Look, what happened on Sunday wasn't supposed to happen," Talia said suddenly. It felt as if she had read my mind.

"Listen Talia, you're exactly like them, whether you want to admit it or not. I don't know what you're trying to accomplish with the It Clique, but keep me out of it, okay?" I said to her firmly.

I wasn't even going to thank her for connecting me with her mom. I got my connections, and I sealed the deal by sneaking out, it was over with. From that

MY MIAMI 1992 – JANUARY (NEW YEAR, NEW DRAMA)

moment, I was going to have zero affiliation with Talia Weaver.

"You know, Chevrolet, I'm actually helping you way more than you think," Talia told me.

"Just leave me alone, Talia!" I said raising my voice, "We can't be friends anymore. I'm done with you."

And with that I walked away and headed back to class before she could say anything. I went back outside to the courtyard (where we were supposed to be before school started) and joined the Volunteer Squad.

"Come on, Jen!" Florence wailed when I joined the group, "Give us the inside scoop on what happened at the Sunday Sneak Out. We won't say a word!"

I still wasn't ready to talk about it.

"Guys, seriously, I don't want to talk about this. I have a lot on my mind right now, I promise I'll tell you next week, when we start working -."

"Volunteering," Lyla corrected me.

"Yeah, I really have to focus on my grades right now," I told them, "I have to ace this math exam."

"We can study with you during lunch in the library," Carolyn said.

"We're not allowed to eat in the library," Florence pointed out.

MY MIAMI 1992 - JANUARY (NEW YEAR, NEW DRAMA)

"Oh well, the good that you put in the world always has a way of coming back to you, so let's help out Jennifer," Carolyn said happily.

I was so grateful for my new friends. They were so eager to sacrifice their lunch time and help me study. Something that the It Clique would never do for me.

*****

When I got home, I decided to take a break from studying and start working on my essay for the Project Author's challenge. I had asked my dad for permission to use his computer (we only had one in our house) for "school research" and he graciously agreed.

The essay was due on Friday, February 28th, (two days after my birthday) and the winners would be announced on the Project's Authors magazine on Sunday, March 1st. The challenge was for all residents of the State of Florida. In addition to winning a cash prize of $10,000, the winner's essay would also be published in the official magazine (which meant you would receive royalties). The contest was such a huge opportunity to turn my family's life around. I *had* to win.

I wasn't sure where to start, so I went upstairs and grabbed my notebook. I flipped to the page where I had written Rayne Benjaminson's address and phone number. I had originally thought about sending a letter, but I decided not to, based on past experiences.

MY MIAMI 1992 - JANUARY (NEW YEAR, NEW DRAMA)

Phone: 888 182 7809
2848 6th Street (Unit 28)
Beaux Bridge, Louisiana, United States of America

I dialed the number from the phone in my dad's office... I almost jumped out of my seat when someone picked up.

"Hi, I'm Haylee Ortega from Rayne Benjaminson's office, how can I help you?" a sweet female voice greeted.

"Hi Haylee, my name is Jennifer, Jennifer Chevrolet. May I please speak to Ms. Benjaminson?" I asked.

"She actually just left her office an hour ago, but can I take a message?"

"Sure!"

I sighed in relief. I hadn't really prepared what I was going to say to Ms. Benjaminson yet.

I informed Haylee that I would like to do a small interview with Rayne Benjaminson, if she'd be willing. Haylee promised to get my message to Ms. Benjaminson. I thanked her profusely and then we hung up.

I stared at the empty word document on the computer. I hadn't written a single paragraph. Even though I wasn't sure how I was going to start my essay, I knew I had to write down something. So, I wrote down a title.

MY MIAMI 1992 - JANUARY (NEW YEAR, NEW DRAMA)

Rayne Benjaminson, From an Outsider's Point of View

```
Hmmm... I was a bit skeptical, but I was
proud that I had at least written down
something!
```

MY MIAMI 1992 - JANUARY (NEW YEAR, NEW DRAMA)

Thursday, January 30th, 1992

At break time in the hallway, I told Lyla, Florence, and Carolyn that I'd be sitting alone at lunch to study. I hadn't done any homework the night before and had gotten yelled at by my science teacher for it. I felt terrible and just wanted to be alone.

Once the lunch period finally came, I was in the corner of the cafeteria minding my own business, when Emerald walked over to me.

"Hey," she said sitting down across from me, "Mind if I sit?"

I groaned internally. I thought I had made it clear that I didn't want to have anything do with the It Clique. Why did they always have to come and bother me!?

"Why can't you just go sit with the It Clique," I said looking at her green eyes.

"I left," Emerald said. "Ever since Talia came along the It Clique has been a mess. Meghan kicked both me and Rosalyn out over the weekend. Charlotte and Skye are the only ones still standing."

"Why did you leave?" I asked curiously.

"Talia. She's so mean to me and the rest of the girls, and she tells Meghan lies about us. So, when Meghan decided to temporarily kick me out for talking back to her, I decided I had enough of it all."

"Wow."

MY MIAMI 1992 - JANUARY (NEW YEAR, NEW DRAMA)

"So, I left. I begged Charlotte to join me, but she refused. She said that she would only leave if Skye did or if she was kicked out," Emerald complained. "It's only a matter of time before Talia gets Charlotte – maybe even Skye – kicked out."

Suddenly I realized what Talia's plan was. She wanted to destroy the It Clique. I finally understood. But one question kept floating in my mind: Why?

I didn't say anything back to Emerald. For the rest of lunch, I studied while she ate her lunch, in complete silence.

It Clique drama was not my problem anymore. I had zero part in it. I needed to pass the math test the next day and I wasn't going to let Emerald's personal drama get in the way.

MY MIAMI 1992 - JANUARY (NEW YEAR, NEW DRAMA)

Friday, January 31st, 1992

That morning, I awoke facing my bedroom wall. When I turned to look at my room, it was still the same as it had been at the beginning of the month. I got up and glanced at the images I'd tacked up – pictures of myself as a baby, my family, my cousins, of Meghan and I…

I stared at the picture of Meghan and I from New Years. I couldn't believe it had only taken a month for Meghan and me to no longer be friends. I removed the photo from my wall. I sighed as I grabbed a box from my closet and placed the picture inside. I was going to replace it with a photo of Lyla, Florence, Carolyn, and I. The same way she had replaced me in her life with Talia.

I walked downstairs. I was bewildered by the fact that the next day would be the start of February 1992. January had flown by. I quickly ate my breakfast while doing some extra studying for my math exam. My stress level was at an all-time high, and it became even higher when my dad asked me to listen to the voicemail replay while he was in the bathroom.

After a few boring advertisement messages, I finally heard one that caught my attention. It was from Hayley, the secretary I had spoken to on Wednesday. I quickly pressed play.

"Hi Jennifer, it's me Haylee from Rayne Benjaminson's office. I just spoke to Ms. Benjaminson, and she will be able to talk

MY MIAMI 1992 - JANUARY (NEW YEAR, NEW DRAMA)

to you tomorrow at 9 am in Louisiana time, so 10 am for you. She's very excited to speak with you again!"

I squealed, went to the phone machine, and quickly deleted the message just in time for my dad to come back from the washroom.

"Hear any important messages?" He asked as he fixed his tie.

"Nope! Just advertisement," I lied effortlessly.

My Dad nodded and went back to his newspaper.

*****

At lunch, I sat alone once more to do more studying since my math exam was immediately after. I was determined to get an A no matter what.

I felt a wave of tension go over me as I was looking down into my math book. I looked up to see Meghan, Skye, and Charlotte hovering over me. Why couldn't the It Clique just leave me alone?

"Why were you talking to Emerald yesterday," Meghan demanded with her hands on her hips.

I looked over at the It Clique table. Talia was sitting eating her lunch quietly and staring over at us. Classic.

"Buzz off, Meghan!" I said looking back into my math book.

MY MIAMI 1992 - JANUARY (NEW YEAR, NEW DRAMA)

I didn't have the time to entertain Meghan's foolishness.

"Don't you dare talk to me that way."

"You're not the boss of me. Go away," I repeated, not even bothering to look up at her.

"You're digging a deep hole for yourself, Jen," Charlotte warned me.

"I don't care. At least I have some purpose around here other than following Meghan around like a robot," I shot back at her. "You're such a hypocrite! Weren't you the one saying all this bad stuff about Meghan on Sunday?"

Guilt swept over me as Meghan turned to Charlotte and looked at her with utter disgust. I felt horrible as I watched tears begin to form in Charlotte's eyes. Meghan was so mean.

"Let's go!" Meghan said to Charlotte; and just as quickly as they came, the It Clique left. Good riddance to bad rubbish!

I sighed and went back to studying.

*****

It was time for the exam, and I was a nervous wreck. Even though I knew I was ready, I was still worried. When I walked into the classroom, I groaned when I noticed the teacher had changed our seating plan.

MY MIAMI 1992 - JANUARY (NEW YEAR, NEW DRAMA)

I originally sat beside Emerald and a boy named Albert, but in the teachers new seating plan I sat right beside Talia at the back of the classroom. Delightful.

I took my seat and ignored Talia as she smugly wished me good luck. I was not going to let her distract me.

When we received the test, I looked at the first question and decided that Mr. Wilson hated me. What type of questions were these?

1. Two angles are _____ angles if their sum is 180 degrees
    a) supplementary
    b) complementary
    c) straight
    d) right

I decided to develop a strategy. I rushed through the easy questions to get them with, to give the harder questions more time. In Mr. Wilson's class, we weren't allowed to submit our tests until the class was over. So, I spent the last ten minutes fiddling with my pencil, correcting questions, and staring at the clock. It was taking forever.

As I was fiddling around quietly, I saw Talia. She was examining my paper… She was cheating off my test!

I looked at her with huge eyes and mouthed, "What are you doing?!"

She rolled her eyes and handed me a note.

MY MIAMI 1992 - JANUARY (NEW YEAR, NEW DRAMA)

Listen up Chevrolet, if you know what's good for you, you'll keep your mouth shut, and not worry about it.

I couldn't believe my eyes. We were both going to get into so much trouble if she was caught. How long had she been copying off my test without me noticing?

I was furious. I had spent that entire week studying, all for Talia to swoop in and take advantage of that and cheat off me. It wasn't fair.

Once the bell rang, I stashed Talia's note in my pocket and handed my test to Mr. Wilson.

I waited for Talia to get out of class, I dragged her arm and brought her to the girls' bathroom nearby. We had a ten-minute break before our next class, so I had just enough time to speak with her.

"Talia. I told you to leave me alone!" I said loudly.

"I am," Talia responded.

"How is cheating off my test, which you should already know could get us both in a lot of trouble, leaving me alone?" I demanded. "I didn't study that hard for this exam, just for you to swoop in and take advantage of it."

"Well, it's the least you could do," Talia shrugged.

"What?"

MY MIAMI 1992 - JANUARY (NEW YEAR, NEW DRAMA)

"You know, for me connecting you to my mom and all."

I couldn't believe the words that were leaving her mouth, "So was the Sunday Sneak Out not enough for you?"

"You're really not that bright, Jennifer Chevrolet," Talia laughed.

"Excuse me?"

"I would have just given you the info about my mom if you had just asked, you know," she explained.

"Talia! I wanted to be your friend first, so it didn't seem like I was just using you. Then the minute I got a chance to finally start talking to you, you replaced me in the It Clique. So don't try to make me look stupid for not going up to you on the first day and asking for your moms personal information," I notified Talia sharply.

Talia stared at herself in the mirror and shuffled her curly hair, "First of all I never replaced you in the It Clique -."

"Listen," I interrupted her, "I don't know or care about what games you're playing with them. Just keep me out of it!"

I walked out of the bathroom and slammed the door shut, leaving Talia inside.

I was going to make Talia admit to cheating before Mr. Wilson found out and got us both

MY MIAMI 1992 - JANUARY (NEW YEAR, NEW DRAMA)

in trouble. I was not going to take any risks when it came to upholding academic integrity. Even if it was at the deficit of Talia. She was going to admit to cheating rather she liked it or not.

*****

After the last class of the day, my dad had called the school to inform Martin and I that he would be late picking us up. So, I decided to wait at the front of the school and read a Rayne Benjaminson book.

I was still reading my novel when Rosalyn and Charlotte came by and sat down two benches away from me. It seemed as if they hadn't noticed that I was even there.

"I hate Talia," Rosalyn said to Charlotte.

"Me too. She's ruining everything," Charlotte agreed.

"I just don't understand why you haven't left."

I knew that it was rude to eavesdrop, but Charlotte and Rosalyn were talking loudly. It was practically impossible not to hear them.

"It's fine actually," Rosalyn said before Charlotte could answer, "I'll tell you more about it when we get to my house but Talia's spreading a crazy rumor about me."

Rosalyn whispered something in Charlotte's ear, and her eyes widened.

MY MIAMI 1992 - JANUARY (NEW YEAR, NEW DRAMA)

I decided to stop listening; eavesdropping was impolite. A part of me was exited to find out what the rumor was and the other was shocked to see Charlotte breaking an IT Clique rule. She was hanging out with Rosalyn, an ex-member of the It Clique. - but at least I knew Charlotte was breaking the It Clique's rules by hanging out with an ex-member.

To avoid overhearing their conversation, I decided to move a couple more benches away from them. As I was sitting, a boy I hadn't met came up and sat beside me.

"Hey, do you know anyone with the name of Jennifer Chevrolet?" he randomly asked me.

"Umm... Yeah, that's me," I replied slowly, "Why?"

"So, you were at the Sunday Sneak Out?"

"Yeah," I sighed. Here we go. Another person who wanted me to spill the tea on what happened.

"Okay, well like I have this friend who is starting a super-secret school drama newspaper. And she wanted me to interview everyone who was at the event. I've already asked Talia, Charlotte, and Rosalyn, but they refused to say anything. Would you mind answering a few questions?"

"What did you want to ask?" I said without thinking.

He took a deep breath, "So there's been a rumor going around that Rosalyn brought

MY MIAMI 1992 - JANUARY (NEW YEAR, NEW DRAMA)

cigarettes to the beach and was trying to force you guys to smoke. Is this true?"

I couldn't believe what I was hearing, "Wait what? Can you say that again?"

He repeated himself then tapped his watch.

It immediately dawned on me why Meghan had kicked Rosalyn out of the It Clique. Talia had probably started the rumor by telling Meghan and Skye. Talia's attempt to make Rosalyn look terrible in front of everyone made no sense whatsoever. What did she have against her? It was an enigma to me.

Then suddenly, I knew how I was going to get Talia to admit to cheating on the math test. I was just about to tell the boy about what had actually occurred on Sunday until I saw my dad's car arrive.

"Listen, meet me right at this exact spot, on Monday at recess, we'll find someplace more private for me to tell you what really happened at the Sunday Sneak Out," I told him.

"Okay, great!"

I stood up and was about to head into my dad's car, but then turned around to ask the boy an important question.

"What did you say your name was again?"

"Caleb," he said with a smile, "Caleb Miller."

MY MIAMI 1992 - JANUARY (NEW YEAR, NEW DRAMA)

"Oh okay, thanks," I got inside the car. I waved goodbye to him, and he waved back.

Caleb Miller... Where had I heard that name before?

*****

Once I got home, I immediately started preparing my questions for my interview with Rayne Benjaminson the next day. I was super grateful that she was willing to take time out of her day to speak with me.

After writing down my questions and practicing saying them confidently saying them confidently, I decided to take time to reflect and write down my February 1992 goals.

February 1992 Goals

- Write a biographical essay for the Project author's challenge.
- Interview with Rayne Benjaminson. Ugh, still not used to that.
- Start Volunteering at the Country Club (NEED TO ASK MOM AND DAD)
- Expose Talia/Make her confess about cheating off my test
- Pay more attention to the Volunteer Squad

I had so much on my hands! It felt as though just "yesterday" Meghan and I were shouting "Happy New Year!" in my living room. Now it was February, both of our birthday months, and we didn't even speak.

MY MIAMI 1992 - JANUARY (NEW YEAR, NEW DRAMA)

I was nervous for the new month, but after all the drama that happened in January, I just knew that there was no way February could top that... Right?

Alright, February 1992, here I come, show me what you've got!

ABOUT THE AUTHOR

Born on April 12th, 2007, in the city of Toronto, Kristina Kasengulu is the author of the series My Miami 1992. When Kristina was just six years old, she moved to Alberta with her mother and younger brother. Her Mom works as a sales associate, while her dad is an engineer in the United States. Kristina wrote the book My Miami 1992 - January (New Year, New Drama) a few days after her 13th birthday (during quarantine) out of inspiration from her own life and the lives of others around her. She is currently 14 years old and in the 9th grade. Although literature is one of her biggest passions, Kristina also enjoys playing instruments at her church, dancing, acting, volunteering, and much more. Although a lot of her persona was portrayed through her main protagonist (Jennifer Chevrolet) she managed to still put tiny bits of herself into each character. She hopes that adolescents will be able to read, learn and be encouraged from her books. One day, by the grace of God, she hopes to become a *#1 New York Times Bestseller*.